THE BEAST OF LONDON

BOOK ONE OF THE MINA MURRAY SERIES

LAUREN GOFFIGAN

Copyright © 2017 by Lauren Goffigan

All rights reserved.

This book or any portion thereof may not be reproduced, or stored in a retrieval system, or transmitted in any form or by any means, electronic, mechanical, photocopying, recording, or otherwise, without the express written permission of the publisher.

This is a work of fiction. Names, characters, organizations, places, events, and incidents are either products of the author's imagination or used fictitiously.

Cover Design by Mibl Art

"One general law, leading to the advancement of all organic beings, namely, multiply, vary, let the strongest live and the weakest die."

- Charles Darwin, *On The Origin of Species*

1

ADVENTURE STORIES

W alking through the streets of the East End, I felt the sudden unnerving sensation of a gaze prickling the back of my neck. I clutched the strap of my bag, scanning my surroundings for any sign of a pursuer. The day was unusually bright and sunny for early May in London, a time when rainfall was more common than sunlight, and the streets around me teemed with the familiar late afternoon sights I had become accustomed to during my daily commutes home from the Halfield Ragged School. Street vendors hawked their wares—kidney pudding, fresh fruit, and ginger beer; flower girls sold bundles of primroses and violets; flocks of eager children crowded around merchants who sold half-penny ices. Passersby weaved around the double deck horse trams, hansom cabs, and carriages that clogged the patchwork of narrow streets.

None of the passersby paid me any mind, and I saw no signs of any potential pursuer, but my unease did not dissipate. I was not far from Whitechapel, where the murderer who called himself Jack the Ripper once lurked. The Ripper had not struck for months, and rumors abounded that he had died or even fled London.

Despite the school's proximity to the Whitechapel murders, I had never before felt unsafe during my commutes. I even lingered in the neighborhood when I visited families who lived in the nearby tenement buildings to give them baked goods I purchased from street vendors, or old books the school no longer needed.

Pushing my disquietude aside, I continued down the street. I simply must have been on edge because of my confrontation with my superior, the schoolmaster Horace Welling, only hours before.

Horace had entered my classroom not long after I dismissed my students for the day, a scowl etched deep into the sharp lines of his face. With his beak-like nose, beady black eyes, and harsh features, Horace reminded me of a crow come to life. I'd overheard my students on many occasions referring to him as such. Though I admonished them for the taunt, I had to fight back an amused smile of my own whenever I did.

Horace had taken an instant dislike to me, and had not spared me a kind word in the three years

I'd taught at the school. If it weren't for the Harkers' influence, I would have never kept my post.

"How may I help you, Mister Welling?" I asked, forcing a polite smile as he approached my desk.

"I overheard you telling the students tales of your past adventures, and I must say I am quite displeased with that method of teaching, Miss Murray. Nonsensical adventure stories are not proper lessons. Whatever you did in your *past* has nothing to do with my curriculum," he said, emphasizing the word 'past' with a slight sneer.

"Children get bored. At times, telling stories is necessary to hold their attention."

"These are some of the poorest children in London. They should be happy to receive an education at all. They do not have the privilege of being bored."

Anger shot through me at his words. Horace was barely middle class, yet his snobbery belonged to someone of the nobility; it was truly insufferable. Usually, I was able to hold my tongue at such remarks, but today had been an exception.

"It is not their fault they were born to a *lower station*," I snapped. "I'm going to give these students the best education I can—the same that I would give to wealthy children. All children enjoy stories. It helps them learn."

Horace's eyes narrowed dangerously. He hated anyone disagreeing with him—especially a female teacher who worked beneath him. He stepped forward, his mouth going tight.

"If you wish to maintain your post, you will adhere to the curriculum I have administered. Otherwise, I am afraid our funding will not be able to continue for your class."

I stared at him in disbelief, but Horace evenly met my eyes. For all his grim-faced dourness and snobbery, Horace was not a cruel man. But I could tell by his expression that he was quite serious.

I calmed myself, setting aside my pride for the sake of the students. Without my class, many of them would be unable to get an education anywhere else, and they would be put to work in the factories . . . or worse.

"All right, Mister Welling," I said, forcing agreeability into my tone. "No more adventure stories. I will stick to the curriculum. My apologies."

Horace's hard mouth curved, settling into what I assumed was his version of a smile.

"I trust we will not need to have such discussions in the future."

"No. Of course not," I replied, though it took every ounce of restraint I had to keep the polite smile pinned on my face.

Looking quite pleased with himself, Horace turned and waddled from the room. As soon as he was gone, my smile vanished, and I wearily leaned back against my desk, taking in the old dusty classroom where I spent much of my time. The school was indeed for the poorest children of the East End, and it showed. My classroom was minuscule in size, dimly lit during the day by sunlight, which filtered through the smudged narrow windows. I had attempted to hide the dirty walls of the classroom with maps and drawings the children made, but the grime was still quite visible. The narrow desks the students shared had become cracked and rickety with age, and the old wooden floors were riddled with splinters.

Despite the decrepit state of the classroom, I had grown fond of it, just as I'd grown fond of my young students. Their joviality and inquisitiveness was infectious, and reminded me of myself at their age. Teaching at the school had become a much-needed refuge, a way to forget the painful events of my past. Dealing with Horace was a minor annoyance in light of such a haven.

I pulled myself from my thoughts and back to the present, though my agreement to not tell any more adventure stories still weighed heavily on my mind. The stories were all about my travels throughout Europe with my father and his former student, Abraham Van Helsing. My father had been a biologist, and I shared his love for the natural sciences. I accompanied him on his travels with Abe around Europe to perform experiments, and he sometimes even managed to sneak me into lectures and conferences. Telling my students embellished versions of our travels had become my way of reliving those happy times. Now I feared that those memories would soon fade to nothing, and I would be left with only the most painful one. The one that still plagued my nightmares.

I paused mid stride as a surge of grief threatened to rise, but I managed to quell it. In the three years since my father's death, I had come to learn that grief was an emotion without end, marked by continual waves of loss and despair that ebbed and flowed for years, like the ocean tides. Perhaps it was best that I could no longer relive my past through those stories. They were a part of my old life; the life I had left behind after Father's death.

As I joined a throng of commuters to approach the Whitechapel and Mile End Underground Station, I noticed a man about fifty yards behind me out of the corner of my eye, moving with slow deliberation to match my pace. This could have been a mere coincidence, but my unease returned and my spine stiffened with alarm. I picked up my pace to push through the slow moving crowd, subtly glancing behind me to see if he would follow suit.

The man picked up his pace as well, and I could feel his intense gaze on me; the same gaze I had sensed only moments earlier.

My instincts had been correct. I was being followed, and I had just identified my pursuer.

I could not fathom who would be following me

or why, but I instinctively felt that I needed to evade him. Not wanting to lead the pursuer to my home, I turned to slip out from the crowd of commuters, bypassing the station to take an abrupt turn down the next street.

The street I had turned onto was isolated and dominated by decrepit lodging houses. A crumbling brick wall marked a dead end. A grave sense of foreboding swept over me as I passed by a butcher shop, which coated the surrounding air with the thick smell of blood.

I hoped that I had lost my pursuer and could turn back around, but I was halfway down the street when I heard steady footfalls behind me.

Taking a deep breath to quell my rising panic, I tried to recall my self-defense training. Years ago, Father had insisted that I undergo self-defense training at a boxing and fencing school just outside of London. As much as I enjoyed physical exercise, I had thought it an odd and unnecessary request, yet he had insisted. I obliged him and took up training under the tutelage of Bradford and Sofia Frances, husband and wife instructors.

If you ever suspect you are being followed, maintain your calm, Sofia had once told me. *Never show your fear. First, you must determine if you are prepared to fight.*

I was unarmed and certainly not prepared to fight. I'd stowed away the two kukri knives Abe had given me as a gift when I started my training. I didn't think I'd ever need them again.

If you are not prepared to fight, find an escape.

I would have to bypass my mysterious pursuer to flee. I was trapped. Behind me, I could hear his steady footfalls as he drew near.

If you cannot escape and you are not prepared to fight . . . do what you must to defend yourself.

I kept walking until I neared the brick wall that closed off the far end of the street, deliberately slowing my pace. The footfalls of my pursuer also slowed as he drew closer still.

I finally stopped walking altogether, keeping my back to him as I pretended to search for something in my bag. Though my heart hammered in my chest and my hands shook violently, I hoped that I appeared calm. I forced myself to wait until the man was close and his hand grasped my shoulder.

"You—"

The word was barely past his lips when I whirled, pulling back from his grip and lifting up my skirt to kick out at his knees. The man let out a startled cry as he crumpled to the ground, and I stepped forward, lifting up my boot and pressing it firmly onto his chest, forcing him onto his back as I glared down at him.

The man was devilishly handsome, with wide cerulean blue eyes that peered up at me from beneath prominent brows. A shade of dark stubble grazed his strong jawline, and wavy chestnut hair fell almost to his shoulders. He did not seem concerned to be flat on his back with my boot on his chest, and quiet amusement danced in his eyes as he met my astonished look with a wry grin.

I stumbled back, reeling with disbelief. It was a face I knew well. A face I thought I would never see again.

Abraham Van Helsing lumbered to his feet, picking up his hat as he pulled himself up to his full height of well over six feet. He grinned down at me, dusting off his vest and black tweed sack coat, and placed his hat securely back on his head. I stared at him, dumbfounded, not quite believing that he was standing before me.

"That was quite the greeting, Mina," he said lightly, in the deeply timbered voice I knew so well, his English only slightly accented by his native Dutch.

"What . . . what are you doing here?" I demanded, when I was finally able to find words. My astonishment rapidly turned into fury. "And why did you follow me like that? You could have called on me at home. You frightened me."

"It was my intention to call on you, but my business at Scotland Yard concluded earlier than I anticipated. When I went to your school you were already leaving; I wanted to see if you recalled your training. I see that you have," he added, with a wry smile. "I am sorry. It was not my intention to frighten you."

I studied him, flushed with an array of conflicting emotions. I was still angry at how he had startled me; but I was also surprised, dismayed, worried, and beneath it all . . . there was a tiny flicker of joy at seeing him again. But as his words broke through my haze of astonishment, the joy dissipated.

"Scotland Yard?" I asked, the pit of my stomach filling with dread. "What business do you have with Scotland Yard? Why are you in London?"

My unease made my tone sharper than I had intended. Abe's casual look of amusement faded, and I caught a fleeting glimpse of hurt in his eyes. But the look was gone as quickly as it had appeared, and he took a step towards me, his face turning grave.

"I have a carriage across the street, we can discuss it there. Please, it is urgent," he added, at my clear hesitation. He stepped forward to tentatively touch my arm, and a rush of heat spread through my skin at his touch.

I took an abrupt step back, and Abe swiftly removed his hand, dropping it to his side. "You have my assurance it will not take long."

I took in his serious expression and the rigid way he held himself. I had rarely seen Abe anxious. His scientific mind focused on facts and rationality rather than the unnerving possibilities of the unknown, and he was usually able to maintain his calm. Whatever he wanted to discuss had to be grave.

"Briefly," I conceded. "And then I must be on my way."

2

THE BEAST OF LONDON

His shoulders relaxed, and I realized that his seemingly casual disposition only served to hide how on edge he truly was. I could now see small lines of tension etched into the skin around his eyes, as well as the faint shadows beneath them.

I fell into step beside him as we turned to head back down the street. When we reached the main thoroughfare of Mile End Road, I glanced around to make sure we weren't noticed, though I knew that no one in the Harkers' social circle would ever set foot in the East End. It would cause quite the scandal if rumors spread that I was in the company of a man who was neither a relative nor my fiancé.

Abe remained silent as we walked, keeping his gaze trained straight ahead. I took in the wide breadth of his shoulders and the long chestnut hair that curled at his nape, far longer than was fashionable for men in London. I tried to ignore the warmth that spread over me at the familiar sight of him, this man I had once loved. He had never been far from my thoughts in the years since our parting, and his physical presence was like a potent memory come to life.

We soon arrived at an ornately decorated carriage, which looked more appropriate for Park Lane or Kensington than the East End; it stood out amongst the shabby buildings and older carriages and cabs that dotted the street.

The driver stepped forward and swung open the door, helping me inside. Abe settled in next to me, and as the driver shut the door behind us, I turned to Abe, acutely aware of our closeness.

"What is so urgent?" I asked.

Abe didn't immediately respond, his eyes so intent on my face that I almost looked away, and he reached for my hand. Stunned, I tried to yank it away, but he held firm, examining my engagement ring—a marquis-shaped ruby surrounded by diamonds on a delicate rose gold band that Jonathan had lovingly slipped on my finger only a few months before. I flushed, feeling oddly guilty as Abe studied it, his eyes unreadable. I yanked my hand out of his, successfully this time, as he met my eyes.

"*Gefeliciteerd,*" he said mildly, congratulating me in Dutch. "I am sorry for not replying to your letter about the engagement; I was traveling in

France at the time for a conference. Jonathan Harker," he continued, and I could now detect a slight trace of contempt in his tone. "You have secured yourself a solicitor from an honorable family. Well done, Mina."

Fiery anger spread through me at his words. Surely my engagement wasn't what he wanted to discuss? I had written to inform him of my engagement when I certainly wasn't obligated to do so, as our own relationship had ended years ago. After all we had been through, shouldn't he wish for my happiness?

I opened my mouth to raise this very point, but stopped myself. There were too many shared wounds between us . . . too much that needed to be left in the past. The three years that had gone by were like an invisible dam that held back the tumult of pain that marked the end of our relationship, and quarreling with him would only cause it to break. I decided to stick to the matter at hand.

"I assume you didn't travel all the way from Amsterdam to mock my engagement," I said instead. "What do you want to discuss?"

"A friend of mine from university summoned me to London. His wife Lucy is suffering from a strange malady. I have thoroughly examined her and I do not believe it is an illness at all—not one with a natural cause," he added, grimly meeting my eyes. "She is exhibiting behavior that we have both heard of before—in Transylvania."

My entire body froze in disbelief. Abe held my gaze for a long moment, allowing time for his disturbing words to settle, before reaching down into a bag resting on the carriage floor, extricating a small stack of documents. He plopped them onto my lap, giving me a sharp nod to indicate that I should read them.

My hands trembled as I picked up the documents and began to rifle through them. They were mostly newspaper clippings, consisting of various headlines:

HORROR IN WHITECHAPEL!

JACK THE RIPPER CLAIMS 5th VICTIM!

THE BEAST OF LONDON STRIKES AGAIN!

GHASTLY MURDER IN THE EAST END!

As I read the headlines, my turmoil increased. Why did he want me to look at these? Like most Londoners, I was well aware of the Whitechapel murders. The Ripper had been in my thoughts only moments earlier when I'd sensed I was being followed.

I looked up at Abe, confused, but there was a quiet insistence in his eyes that urged me to continue. I looked back down, continuing to flip through the newspaper clippings, until I arrived at a grisly photograph.

The photo was of a crime scene. A young woman lay dead on the dingy floor of a lodging house. Her throat had been violently torn out, her eyes wide and unseeing. A wave of nausea rose in my stomach as an image from my memories replaced the image from the photo—an image from my nightmares.

The forest. The rain. The unseeing eyes of Father.

I shut my eyes, roughly shoving the documents back at him.

"An immigrant family of ten residing in a lodging house in Whitechapel vanished last night. The only person left behind was this poor young woman. I have a contact at Scotland Yard who is on the team that investigated the Ripper murders. He is the one who gave me this photograph. There are—"

"Why did you want me to see these? Everyone in London—in Europe—knows about the Ripper. And what does this have to do with Mister Holmwood's wife?" I demanded.

"You know exactly why," Abe replied. "I need you to listen to me. We know your father was likely investigating the—"

"And look what happened to him," I interrupted bitterly. I expelled a sharp breath and closed my eyes, pressing my shaky fingers to my temples. His words were bringing back dark and painful memories that I desperately wanted to forget.

"I am sorry, I do not mean to upset you. But I believe that you and I may be the only ones in London who have seen this before. We could perhaps help the—"

"No," I said, reaching past him to rap on the carriage window. "I told you years ago I want nothing to do with any of this. Had Father never gone to Transylvania, he would still be alive. Now let me out."

"Let us at least take you home."

"I prefer to walk."

Abe studied me, quiet frustration and something else I couldn't identify lurking in his eyes. He finally turned away from me, reaching out to open the carriage door and stepping out. I hastily climbed out after him, waving away both his and the driver's offer of help.

"Mina—" Abe began, when we were once again facing each other.

"Please do not contact me about this again," I said, looking away from the distress in his eyes. It was an echo of our parting years ago, and my chest tightened at the memory. "Goodbye."

I didn't dare look back as I walked away, and to my relief he did not try to stop me.

When I reached Highgate, I was still disconcerted. Walking along High Street, I tried to focus on the trees that lined Waterlow Park as they danced with the late afternoon breeze, a sight which usually filled me with tranquility. But the sight had no effect as I recalled both Abe's words and the lifeless eyes of the woman from the photograph.

She is exhibiting behavior that we have both heard of before—in Transylvania.

Two years prior to my father's death, we had journeyed to the Transylvanian countryside to observe the abundant animal and botanical species native to the Carpathian mountains. The villagers in the region told us supernatural tales of evil spirits that lurked in the surrounding mountains. When they told us of bodies viciously torn apart or drained of blood, we had assumed there was a rational explanation, and dismissed their tales as superstitions born of ignorance. But the villagers persisted with their tales, and they had many names for the preternatural creature they thought was responsible. *Strigoi. Blutsauger. Kisertet.*

Vampire.

Fear stirred in me, but I pushed it aside, unearthing the house keys from my bag as I turned on to my street. Such a creature did not exist—could not exist. I still did not know exactly what I'd seen the night of Father's death. My vision had been distorted through a fog of shock and grief. Abe had no right to try and pull me back into our shared gruesome past, as if it were something to which I would forever be entwined. I had slowly been untangling myself from the cords of the past... day by day, year by year. What had happened in Transylvania was far behind me, and there it would remain.

I arrived at my front door and unlocked it. Stepping into the entrance hall, I welcomed the sense of calm that settled over me.

After Father's death, I had worried that living in the home I grew up in and shared with him would be too painful. But my home provided a comforting familiarity I needed in the early days of my bereavement. It was a four-story terraced home, its walls adorned with paintings of nature that Father had inherited from his own family or purchased, as well as framed copies of scientific drawings of plant and animal species that I'd done for his publications. The wide windows in most of the rooms let in an abundance of light, even on the most dreary days. I would truly miss it when I moved into Jonathan's Mayfair home after we were wed.

I smiled at the thought of Jonathan. I would not let Abe's visit mar the rest of my day. I was to have dinner with Jonathan and his mother later. He could always tell when I was upset, and I was uncertain that I even wanted him to know about Abe's appearance today.

"Mina? Are you all right?"

Clara stepped out of the drawing room, frowning as she studied my anxious features with motherly concern.

Clara had worked as a housekeeper for my

family since I was a small child, but she seemed ageless to me. Her warm brown eyes, strong features, and long, graying brunette hair that she wore in an ever-present bun had hardly changed over the years. She started not long after my mother's death, and she was the closest person in my life that I had to a mother. She was well aware of the tragic past Abe and I shared, and I knew it would only cause her great worry if she were to know of his visit.

"Yes. Just trouble with Horace again," I lied, forcing a smile. But I was unable to meet her eyes. I could never truly lie to Clara; a half-truth would have to do. Clara stepped forward to collect my bag, her mouth narrowing into a thin line of dislike at the mention of Horace.

"He should be grateful ta have you. You don't even need ta teach there," she said, scowling.

"I like teaching there," I returned, with a patient smile, moving past her towards the stairs at the side of the entrance hall.

My father had earned good wages as a professor at Cambridge, but he had a large inheritance from his family that he'd barely touched during his lifetime. As an only child, his home and inheritance all went to me. But I intended to keep teaching, and Jonathan had raised no objection when I informed him that I'd like to keep working after we were wed, something unheard of in his family.

As I started up the stairs, a sudden urge came over me, and I turned back towards Clara.

"Where are the keys to Father's study?"

"In t' top desk drawer int' library. Why do you —" Clara began, looking at me with surprise. I never went into Father's study.

"I need one of his maps for a lesson plan," I interrupted, avoiding her probing look. I hated how the lies were increasing, but if she pushed for details, I would be forced to tell her of Abe's visit, and I refused to worry her. I hurried up the stairs before she could question me further, though I could feel her puzzled eyes on my retreating back.

Ever since his death, I had taken to avoiding Father's study. Father had spent many long hours there, and when I was a child I'd often rush in, wrapping my arms around his legs and begging him to read to me. On the days when Clara had not whisked me off with hushed admonishments, he would indulge me, swinging me up into his arms as he told me tales of lands that seemed so far away and exotic to my young mind—whether they were nearby countries such as France, Germany, or the Low Countries, or faraway lands like India or the Americas. *When I travel to these places*, he had once promised, leaning in close as my eyes went wide with excitement. *You'll come with me, poppet.*

I halted in my tracks as I reached the door to his study, blinking back the tears that pricked at my eyes, until I forced myself to unlock the door and step inside.

The lone window in the room was covered by thick curtains, so I lit the gas lamp next to the door, and the room filled with a soft and hazy light. The study looked as it had for years: brimming with books, journals, drawings and maps. But everything was now coated in a thick layer of dust; it had the look of a room frozen in time.

I had forbidden Clara to clean or touch anything in the study until I could sort through Father's things. But the pain that filled me every time I entered the study had been too overwhelming, and though years had passed, I still had not done so.

I entered the room further, approaching the desk. I opened the top drawer, picking up the spectacles that rested inside. Since he frequently lost them, Father had kept several pairs of spectacles. He had left this pair behind right before his last trip. Still clutching them in my hands, I reached down to pick up a framed photograph inside the drawer, covered in dust. I blew the dust away, and studied it.

In the photo, Father sat in this very study, a handsome and gay man in his fifties, staring politely at the camera. He had been tall and robust, with laughing brown eyes and the dark curly hair that I'd inherited. I lovingly traced my fingers over the image of his face, and this time I allowed my tears to fall as grief seized me once more.

After several moments, I wiped my eyes and placed the photograph and spectacles back in the drawer, firmly reminding myself why I'd come into the study.

I reached further into the drawer, searching for Father's most recent journal. It was not in the rear of the drawer where he usually kept it. Frowning, I searched the other drawers, but it was nowhere to be found.

It was missing.

3

THE HARKERS

Later that evening, as I sat in the opulent dining room of my future mother-in-law's home, Father's missing journal was still on my mind. Clara had assured me that she hadn't removed anything from the study. I told myself that the journal could simply be with his other belongings that I had stored in the cellar, or that it had been misplaced at some point during the last three years. But my disquietude lingered, and I had to force a polite smile as Mary droned on about wedding invitations.

I shifted in my tightly corseted gown of lavender silk, an outfit much smarter than the simple cotton dresses I wore to school. But dinners at Mary Harker's home were never less than formal affairs, even when it was just me, Jonathan, and Mary. I suspected that Mary used the dinners as an opportunity to both show off her wealth and subtly remind me that I would be expected to carry on the tradition of hosting elaborate dinners after Jonathan and I were wed.

I pretended to listen to Mary, picking at my meal of mulligatawny soup, roast chicken, potatoes and damson pudding, sliding a glance across the narrow dining room table towards my fiancé.

Jonathan was youthfully attractive, with dark hair and expressive hazel eyes that shifted from light brown to green depending on his mood, and a generous mouth that seemed to always border on a smile. He usually gave me sympathetic looks or sly winks during the long arduous dinners with his mother. But now he looked distracted, his gaze intent on the elaborate floral arrangement in the center of the table as he absently sipped his wine.

"We must invite the Crawfords, they will certainly expect us to do so," Mary said, delicately dabbing at her lips with a napkin. "I expect you have no objections, Mina?"

Her smile was as forced as mine as she looked at me, her eyebrows raised as she waited for my reply. Mary disapproved of me, and she did a poor job of hiding it. Before our engagement, Jonathan had been one of the most eligible bachelors in London. His deceased father had been a wealthy barrister, and Jonathan was the sole heir to his fortune. I was certain Mary had a slew of society women in mind to wed her son before he chose me, the daughter of a social outcast by choice, who fit nowhere in the stratified society to which the esteemed Harker family belonged. It didn't seem to matter to her that I had an inheritance of my own, and though I had tried many times to fall into her favor, I soon realized that I would never be the type of woman she wanted her son to marry. Now, for Jonathan's sake, we simply endured each other.

"None at all," I returned with stiff politeness. I didn't know who the Crawfords were, but I suspected they were another stuffy family well acquainted with Mary Harker.

Thus far, Jonathan and I had made only vague plans for our wedding, and we only recently set a date for next spring. Mary was consistently suspicious of my lack of interest in the wedding, especially considering that I was twenty-five and creeping towards spinsterhood in her opinion. *It is a woman's only day*, she would often chide, studying me with narrowed eyes.

For Mary's sake, I tried to appear enthusiastic about my upcoming wedding, not wanting to reveal that I found the pomp of society weddings silly and quite unnecessary. As a girl, I never dreamed of getting married—my only desire then was to become an adventurer and a scientist. But I pushed those dreams aside after Father's death. Now, I just wanted to teach and have a quiet life with Jonathan, and an elaborate wedding simply did not matter to me.

"Wonderful," Mary said, her eyes still trained on me. "We have not discussed what you plan to do about your teaching position after you are wed. When do you plan to leave your post?"

I tensed, and her words seemed to pull Jonathan from his distracted thoughts. He looked at his mother with a frown.

"What do you mean, Mother?" he asked.

"Our Mina can hardly work at that . . . school, once she is married," Mary sniffed, her nose crinkling in disgust at the very thought of the school where I taught. "If she insists on teaching, we can have her placed at a private one in a better neighborhood. Perhaps one here in Kensington—or Mayfair. I worry about my future daughter-in-law traveling to the East End every day," she added, her hand straying to her heart in an exaggerated gesture of concern. But Mary was a terrible liar; her words were blatantly insincere.

"Mother . . ." Jonathan began, his voice tight with warning.

"I'm sorry, darling," Mary said, not sounding at all apologetic. "I just hear the most terrible rumors about those—what are they called? *Ragged* schools? For poor children? I think it is rather noble that she chose to teach there, but once Mina is officially a Harker—"

"The school is quite understaffed," I said, trying to hide my irritation behind a smile. "And I enjoy teaching the children there. It's hardly their fault they were born poor."

"Oh, I agree. But as Jonathan's wife, you can hardly be expected to—"

"Mina is happy teaching where she is. If she is happy, then so am I," Jonathan interjected.

A rush of love and gratitude towards Jonathan swirled within me, and I gave him a small smile, which he returned. Jonathan shared none of the snobbery that his mother and others of his class wore with pride. Mary bristled, irritated by our solidarity.

"Very well," she said, though I knew the matter was hardly settled as far as she was concerned. "Will you be able to join me for tea this Sunday afternoon, Mina? I want to discuss more wedding details."

I involuntarily stiffened. My Sunday afternoons were either spent with Jonathan taking walks around a different part of the city, or reading at home with a cup of tea. I enjoyed my Sunday afternoons. The thought of spending it with Mary and the haughty society women she often invited filled me with dread. With all of the turbulent emotions that had swirled through me since Abe's reappearance, I needed an afternoon of relaxation.

My reluctance didn't escape Mary's notice. Nothing did, unfortunately. She raised an eyebrow.

"Is there a problem, my dear? You have been

engaged to my son for six months, and you have only just set a date. People are beginning to talk."

"Well, then we should wed right away. We certainly would not want people to talk," I coolly returned.

Though it was somewhat satisfying to see Mary's angry flush at my retort, I felt a twinge of regret. I didn't need to deepen Mary's disapproval of me. Mary scowled, and even Jonathan gave me a slightly disapproving frown.

"I'm sorry, Mary," I said hastily, giving her as warm of a smile as I could muster. "I've had a bit of a stressful day. Tea on Sunday would be lovely."

Mary nodded, but she still looked greatly offended. I turned to give Jonathan an apologetic look, but his focus had returned to the tablecloth, and he again seemed to be lost in his own thoughts.

The remainder of the meal was brief. I tried to engage Mary in conversation, inquiring about the many social functions she was to attend over the course of the next month. I even made suggestions for wedding decorations, but Mary offered only stilted replies.

I was relieved when the meal came to an end. Jonathan embraced and kissed his mother farewell; she stiffly offered me her cheek to kiss.

The air outside was damp with the promise of rain, but we still decided to take a brief walk before Jonathan escorted me back to Highgate. A light fog had descended over the Kensington streets, battling with the numerous gas lamps to cloak the neighborhood with its own form of hazy luminescence. In spite of the threat of rain and the increasing lateness of the hour, the streets still bustled with activity, and we had to navigate our way past other couples and passersby.

As we began our walk, I took Jonathan's offered arm, glancing up to take in his profile. I met Jonathan at a charity ball over a year ago, where he had quietly mocked the exaggerated accents of the aristocratic guests, eliciting a genuine laugh from me for the first time in months. Our courtship had begun tentatively, with long talks in Mary's drawing room. Mary had insisted on serving as our chaperone since both of my parents were deceased and I had very little contact with my father's extended family. Our talks soon transitioned into lengthy walks all around London, and I found myself looking forward to our time together.

I had told him about Father, our travels, and my love of the sciences; careful to leave out details of exactly what we'd encountered in Transylvania, merely telling him that Father's death was a tragic accident. To my relief, he had not pressed for more details, innately seeming to understand how painful Father's death was for me—he'd lost his own father not long before our courtship began.

Jonathan told me of his work as a solicitor, and how his mother wanted him to become a barrister like his late father, but he took greater joy in helping the less privileged. His firm specialized in handling estate transactions for wealthy clients to purchase housing all throughout London for the poor.

I fell in love with Jonathan quite against my will. My grief over Father's death and my long time love for Abe still hovered in the back of my heart, never letting me forget that they were there. Jonathan was not dismayed by my unconventional past, nor by my outsider status in society because of it. *You are unlike anyone I have ever met*, he'd said earnestly, before kissing me for the first time. When he proposed to me during a rainy carriage ride down Piccadilly, there was only one response I could possibly give him. I knew that with Jonathan, I would finally be able to move forward with my life and leave the tragedy in my past behind. *Yes*, I had tremulously whispered to him. *With all my heart, yes*.

"I'm sorry I was cross with your mother," I said to him now. "I don't think she accepted my apology. I'll call on her tomorrow, if that would—"

"We both know my mother. There is no need to offer any additional apologies, my darling."

He gave me a gentle smile, but he still looked vaguely troubled.

"Is something wrong, Jonathan? You've been distracted all evening." Had someone spotted me and Abe earlier today? Was that what was troubling him? Jonathan stopped mid-stride and turned to face me, his eyes shadowed with anxiety. I stood stiffly, bracing myself for his response.

"Someone broke into our offices last night," he said. "It was completely destroyed when I arrived this morning, yet nothing was taken."

"No," I breathed, frowning with concern.

"Last week I discovered a few files missing," Jonathan continued, his brow furrowing. "After what happened today, I'm wondering if the two incidents are related. Peter told me that if there are any further incidents, we might have to move offices. He's starting to think London's become too dangerous."

"I'm sorry," I said sympathetically. Peter Hawkins was Jonathan's partner at their two-man firm, a kind man in his fifties who shared Jonathan's charitable nature, and whom I liked very much. "Is there anything I can do?"

"You can walk with me along the river," he said with a smile, reaching out to pull me in close to his side. "Your presence is all that I require."

I returned his smile, and we made our way south through Kensington towards the Thames. Once we reached the walking path that ran along the river, Jonathan pulled me in even closer, and I rested my head on his shoulder.

"I have been so distracted that I've neglected you, darling. How are you? Is Horace giving you any trouble?" Jonathan asked, raising my hand to his lips to give it a loving kiss.

I hesitated. Now would be the ideal time to tell him about Abe's visit. Jonathan knew that Abe traveled with me and Father, but he had never inquired about the exact nature of our relationship. I suspected that he didn't want to know.

"Mina?" Jonathan persisted.

As with Clara, I decided that I didn't want to cause Jonathan undue concern. He had enough on his mind with the incidents at his office. *Abe's visit was inconsequential*, I told myself. *I will not be seeing him again.*

"Horace scolded me today for telling adventure stories to the children," I said, forcing a wry but annoyed smile, ignoring my guilt at the purposeful evasion. "He can be truly insufferable. But I love those students. I endure him for their sake."

"Your students are lucky to have you. I meant what I said to Mother about your teaching. But I do confess . . ." he began, his words trailing off into silence as he looked away.

"What?"

"With all the traveling you've done; the life you led before . . . I fear you would be terribly bored as a solicitor's wife," he confessed.

Jonathan had expressed such concerns before, though I had repeatedly assured him otherwise. I wanted nothing of the life I had lived before I met him. I set aside my annoyance at this repeated concern; in light of the day's events, I didn't want to quarrel with him.

I stopped walking, turning him to face me as I gave him a look of mock offense.

"You are hardly just a solicitor, Jonathan. You perform the best impressions of anyone in London, and I get to be your solo audience."

My words had their intended effect, and Jonathan laughed. I smiled, reaching up to gently touch his face.

"I love you, Jonathan Harker. My place is here with you."

I cast a hasty look around to ensure we were alone before boldly reaching up to kiss him. Jonathan responded, and we only pulled away when we heard the footfalls of another approaching couple.

We continued along the path in companionable silence, periodically stopping to exchange kisses whenever we were alone. During one particularly passionate kiss, it began to rain. Jonathan pulled away from me with great reluctance, looking up at the dark and cloudy sky.

"We can find a cab," he suggested.

"No. . . I rather enjoy walking in the rain. And some of our best memories are from walking in the rain," I added, with a nostalgic smile. "Remember our walk home from the museum?"

"Of course," he said, feigning a grimace as he wound his fingers through mine. "The best and the worst day."

Jonathan had not only proposed to me in the

rain, he'd also told me he loved me for the first time during a downpour. We had decided to make the long walk back to my home after taking in an exhibition of drawings at the British Museum, when there was a sudden torrential downpour of rain halfway through our walk. Unable to find a cab, we had hurried to the nearest Underground station, our clothing soaked straight through. Ignoring the disapproving gazes of other passengers as we dripped all over the floors of the train, we took in our mutually drenched states and began to laugh.

"I–I love you, Mina," Jonathan had said suddenly, as our laughter subsided. An embarrassed flush spread over his cheeks at both my look of astonishment and the other passengers' stares.

"I love you too," I had replied, and he looked greatly relieved as his flush faded. Out of the corner of my eye, I saw many of the other passengers smile at our exchange. As soon as we emerged from the station, we found an isolated side street, where Jonathan passionately kissed me.

"Clara was quite cross with you when I returned home," I said now, smiling at the memory as we left the walking path to head back towards Kensington. I cleared my throat and did my best impression of Clara's Yorkshire accent. "'I thought he was from a gran' family. Takin' a lady out int' pourin' rain.'"

"Ah, but we both know that you are not a

typical lady. The walk home was your idea," Jonathan protested, with playful defensiveness.

"Perhaps," I returned, with a sly grin.

When we arrived in Highgate, the light rain had tapered off. We walked hand in hand up the stairs to my front door, and Jonathan turned to look at the dark windows of my home, frowning.

"I worry about you here all alone."

"I'm hardly alone. Clara is often here," I said. "We could elope, and I could move into your home sooner . . ." I added, with a mischievous smile.

"Mother would have a heart attack." Jonathan laughed, looking both horrified and amused at the same time. "Darling, I *want* to show you off as my bride. The wait will be worth it."

My anxiety over Abe's reappearance did not dissipate the next day, and I had to force myself to concentrate on my students as they took turns reading aloud from their grammar books.

I had gently informed them that we would stick to Horace's curriculum going forward, and I would not be telling any more adventure stories. My anger towards Horace reawakened when I saw the disappointment on their young faces. My tales of the world outside London was likely the only chance they'd ever have of experiencing it. My own pleasure aside, I loved seeing the light in their eyes as I described seeing the canals of Amsterdam, the multitude of evergreens in the Black Forest of Germany, and the vast Carpathian Mountain range.

By the end of the school day, the students were more muted than usual, and I noticed a few struggling to keep their eyes open as I had them recite their vocabulary tables. When I dismissed them for the day, they filed out without their usual cheery goodbyes, and I watched them leave with a concerned frown. I would have to find another way to make the lessons enjoyable.

As I took the Underground back to Highgate, my thoughts drifted to Abe rather than lesson plans. He was persistent, and I sincerely doubted that he had left London. He had once convinced the stubborn leader of a biology conference in Paris to allow me entrance by convincing him I was a distant relative of the queen. I couldn't help but smile at the memory.

Tonight I was to attend a London Law Society ball with Jonathan. I knew that I needed to clear my mind, hurry home and get dressed, but when I reached Highgate, I found myself walking into the lush green grounds of Waterlow Park, heading towards a place I had not visited in months.

4

THE BALL

The park was quiet, with only a few men and women strolling by or lounging on the various benches that dotted the grounds. By the time I reached the far edge of the park, the only sounds of humanity were the distant clopping of horse hooves and grind of carriage wheels, along with the faint voices of vendors selling their wares at the markets on High Street.

I soon reached my destination at the far end of the park, Highgate Cemetery. Ignoring the tendrils of dread that coiled around my chest, I made my way past the front gates, heading down a long dusty path that snaked through the cemetery grounds. The silence of the cemetery was as deafening as any noise, and as I walked past the multitude of gothic tombstones, it seemed as if the dead watched me in silent solemnity.

I reached the edge of the path, taking the left

fork onto a narrower path until I arrived at a pair of simple granite headstones. I sank to my knees before them, a heaviness settling over me as I reached out with shaking fingers to trace the engraved words.

ROBERT MURRAY, BELOVED HUSBAND AND FATHER

I dropped my hand, reaching out to touch the engraved words of the adjacent headstone.

EVA MURRAY, BELOVED WIFE AND MOTHER

I had never truly known my mother. When I was a child of five, she'd left England after a long illness to seek further treatment in Italy. Her ship sank and her body had been lost at sea. I don't believe Father ever fully recovered from her loss.

I had precious few memories of her. I could remember that she was beautiful, with long dark hair that I would wrap around my small hands as she laughed, and wide brown eyes that radiated both warmth and sadness. Father didn't speak of her often, and a great shadow fell over his face whenever I inquired about her. Though I was too young when she died to feel her loss the way I felt Father's, the ache of her missing presence had always been there. I reached up to touch the gold spinner locket around my neck. It contained a small photograph of me seated on her lap as a child, a gift she had given me shortly before she died.

A strange sensation on the back of my neck pulled me from my thoughts, and I went still. It was the feeling of a cold gaze searing my skin; an odd bite of frost amidst the warmth of the day. But this sensation felt different than that of the day before; there was an immediate sense of ominous danger.

I stumbled to my feet, looking around at the empty cemetery grounds, almost hoping to see Abe. There was no one else here, but my instincts told me to leave. I hurried back down the path, still feeling that persistent and haunting sensation of being watched.

I was still on edge when I returned home, and though I knew I needed to get dressed for tonight's ball, I spent a good hour searching through Father's study and the cellar for any sign of his missing journal. It wasn't until Clara entered the cellar to inform me that Jonathan would shortly arrive that I reluctantly gave up the search.

"Why are you lookin' for your father's journal?" Clara asked curiously, as she helped me lace up my corset in front of my bedroom mirror moments later. "You've not looked through his things in years."

"He has notes that I could use for my lessons," I lied, avoiding Clara's perceptive scrutiny. Once she secured my corset, I abruptly moved away from her, picking up the evening gown that I was to wear, still not looking at her. "I can finish getting dressed on my own. I don't want you to miss your train."

Clara lived in Luton, in a small home that once belonged to Father's family, which he'd gifted to her in his will. But Clara often slept here in her old room, especially in the months after Father's death. It was only after Jonathan and I began courting that she started to spend more time in her own home.

"I'm stayin' overnight ta receive t' bread delivery tomorrow. I told you earlier," Clara said, her voice shadowed with concern.

"Right. Of course," I said, letting out a forced laugh as I put on my petticoat.

"Mina," Clara said, in an authoritative tone that I recalled from my childhood, and I instinctively looked up. She was regarding me with a worried frown. "Is everythin' all right?"

"You know how much I hate these society balls," I said, giving her what I hoped was a genuine smile. "I'd much rather stay home and read."

Clara knew me too well, and I could tell that she didn't believe me. But she said nothing, merely stepping forward to help me into my gown. When I was completely dressed and ready to go, she scented my skin with lavender perfume and handed me my cloak and silk gloves.

"There," Clara beamed, stepping aside to allow me to take in my reflection.

The woman who stared back at me was dressed in a ball gown of fine red muslin adorned with symmetrical black lace garnitures at the sleeves and bodice. Her long dark curls were tucked back into a fashionable bun, her cheekbones and full mouth dabbed with a blood red pomade. Her eyelashes had been darkened with elderberries, highlighting her wide amber eyes. She looked very much like a woman of London society; soon to be an official member of the Harker family. She didn't look like me at all.

I turned away from my reflection, feeling like an actress who was dressed for a part in a play, about to take her place on stage. Indeed, whenever I attended one of these balls, I felt as if I were putting on a performance. Though Jonathan shared my disdain for such affairs, he always blended in perfectly, effortlessly engaging in polite conversation, while I struggled to follow all the rules of etiquette. *Do not speak too loudly. Do not cross the ballroom unattended. Do not speak unless invited to, when spoken to, only offer brief replies.* There were many more that I had been forced to learn; Mary had practically given me a course in ball etiquette after Jonathan and I were engaged.

I began to tug on the gloves. Clara stopped me, tightly gripping both my hands in hers.

"I'm here for you if you need ta talk," she said, searching my eyes.

I hesitated, tempted to tell her about Abe's visit and the sense of being watched at the cemetery, but there was a knock at the door before I could speak. Clara reluctantly released my hands, leaving the room to answer it, and I watched her go. Guilt lingered in me because I had not confided in her, though I assured myself it was for the best.

Jonathan had arrived in the Harker family carriage. He looked dashing in a black tailcoat with a white bow tie and winged collar. He bid Clara a warm farewell and kissed me softly before escorting me into the carriage. The carriage lurched and jolted over the streets as it made its way towards the Langham Hotel in the West End.

"You look lovely, darling," he said. "How will I distract myself from your beauty tonight?"

"Perhaps playing our game will help," I replied, with a teasing smile.

I was relieved that he had returned to his usual cheerful self, and I was determined to enjoy my evening with him, casting aside the dark thoughts that had plagued me since Abe's visit. Jonathan and I had invented a game of sorts every time we attended a society ball. We would keep track of how many times someone dropped the name of a royal or aristocrat in order to impress the listener, how many times someone would fail some arbitrary rule of etiquette, how many times someone looked quietly horrified when they learned that I was the daughter of Robert Murray and never had an official coming out. Our game made balls more tolerable, if not somewhat enjoyable.

The carriage slowed to a crawl as it joined a slew of other carriages approaching the Langham, a sprawling beehive of a building that dominated the narrow street it occupied. Our carriage pulled to a complete stop near the crowded entrance of the hotel, and after our driver opened the door for us, we joined the stream of guests that flooded through the grand entrance and into the massive gilded lobby, which was illuminated with the glare of electric lights. We continued through the lobby with the other guests, reaching the cloak and hat rooms.

As Jonathan headed towards the hat room, I entered the cloakroom. The room was a sea of color and fabric as the female guests took off their cloaks and handed them off to patiently waiting maids. After I handed my own cloak off to a shy young maid, I heard my whispered name and felt several pairs of eyes on me.

I turned, spotting a group of women hovering by the exit. They stopped whispering amongst themselves when I turned, staring at me with open disdain. I recognized the woman who seemed to be their default leader, a sour-faced blonde dressed in an extravagant gown of pale lavender silk.

I had encountered Jane Newton at several society functions. Like Mary, her dislike of me was plain, but I suspected it was born more from jealousy than my reputation. Her family was well acquainted with the Harkers, and it was quite obvious that she had expected Jonathan to court and propose to her. The fact that he had chosen such a social outcast for his bride only added to the insult.

Taking a deep breath, I moved towards them, silently noting with pleasure their discomfort at my approach.

"I'm already acquainted with Miss Newton," I said politely, addressing Jane's cohorts. "I'm Mina Murray."

The women remained stiff for a moment, but the manners that had been ingrained into each of them since birth took hold, and they stiffly gave me nods of greeting.

"It is lovely to see you again, Miss Murray," Jane lied. "I never had the opportunity to formally congratulate you on your engagement to Mister Harker."

"Thank you," I returned, as she held my even gaze with her venomous one.

"May I ask you something?" she asked, taking a step forward as she dramatically lowered her voice. "Is it true that your father was Robert Murray—that Cambridge professor who went mad and died pursuing one of his theories? How terribly tragic."

A hot burst of rage exploded in my chest at her words, and I clenched my hands into fists at my sides. Jane's lips curled into a cheap imitation of a sympathetic smile, and the women around her could barely stifle their own smug smiles. I knew Jane was purposefully trying to upset me; she knew exactly who my father was.

"My fiancé has spoken of you many times, Miss Newton," I said calmly, deciding not to acknowledge her cruel inquiry. "He described you as a rather vapid childhood friend of his who loved him deeply. He told me he only felt pity for you."

This time, I had to suppress a smile of pleasure as Jane's eyes snapped with fury, her smile freezing on her face. Her friends were silent with shock at my insult.

"It was a pleasure, Miss Newton. I will share your well wishes with my fiancé. We will send out wedding invitations quite soon. I look forward to seeing you at our wedding."

I gave them a bright smile before turning to leave the cloakroom. As satisfying as it was to deliver the final verbal blow, her words about Father still stung, and I needed a moment to calm myself before stepping back out into the corridor.

I was still shaken as I moved towards the entrance of the hat room to rejoin Jonathan. Father had become estranged from the wealthy family he was born into when he opted to pursue a life of science rather than work in the family business of finance, and I had only met his extended family on several occasions. He had made an active choice to not participate in society events, finding them stuffy and austere, and I never had my formal coming out. He didn't have many close friends when he died, and there had been very little mourning from society after his death.

I was no stranger to the rumors that ran rampant regarding his mysterious death in Transylvania, and it should have been no surprise to me that the society he shunned in life had turned its back on him in death. But the general apathy regarding his death still stung.

And now, a tiny voice in the back of my head mocked, *you've become a part of the society that he so despised.*

I ignored the thought, and managed a bright smile when Jonathan stepped out of the hat room, taking my arm to escort me towards the ballroom. I knew if I told Jonathan about Jane's insult he would insist on confronting her, and I didn't want her to mar our entire evening.

We entered the ballroom, where several ornate chandeliers hung from the ceiling in a long row, flooding the ballroom with dazzling electric light. Gold-edged pillars lined the walls, and the floor-to-ceiling windows were draped with curtains of fine gold gossamer to match the grandeur of the pillars. The tables, draped with tablecloths of intricate lace, were pushed to the side, allowing ample room for the guests to mingle and dance, and some guests had already begun to move towards the dance floor. At the far end of the room, an orchestra played the opening strains for the first dance of the evening, a waltz.

After we made brief introductions with some of the guests, Jonathan led me out onto the dance floor. As we danced, I focused only on Jonathan, and all thoughts of Jane Newton soon faded away.

The orchestra switched to a quadrille, and we reluctantly released each other to dance with other couples. By the end of the third dance, Jonathan took my arm and we moved towards the tables on the far edges of the ballroom for a break.

"I counted three," Jonathan said in a low voice, as we took our seats. "The wife of the barrister I danced with mentioned that she had her coming out at the queen's court—three times."

"You're already ahead of me," I replied with mock disappointment. "My dance partners were perfectly mute. That is hardly fair."

"The night has just begun, darling. There are plenty of other dances," Jonathan said with a smile. Disregarding all rules about public displays of affection, he lifted my gloved hand to his lips and placed a kiss on my wrist.

"Jonathan?"

Flushing, I placed my hand back in my lap, looking up as Peter Hawkins approached us, his anxious eyes focused only on Jonathan.

"I apologize for my interruption, but there's an urgent manner I need to discuss with you," Peter said, giving us both an apologetic smile before his eyes once again settled on Jonathan. "You should find a gentleman to dance with your fiancée."

"If anyone asks me to dance, I will happily oblige him," I said quickly, though I dreaded the thought of being stuck in conversation with some stuffy barrister.

"I'll return presently," Jonathan said, squeezing my hand before getting to his feet to leave with Peter.

I studied them with mild concern as they left, wondering what Peter wanted to discuss so urgently at this hour. The orchestra switched back to a waltz, and I relaxed in my seat as the couples on the dance floor moved into formation.

A tall male figure suddenly appeared in front of me, and I nervously looked up, expecting to see said stuffy barrister.

I froze when I saw who stood before me. Looking uncomfortable in his long black waistcoat, Abe extended a hand towards me, his expression quietly exigent.

"May I have the pleasure of this dance?"

I stared at Abe in disbelief. Once my initial shock passed over his second abrupt appearance, I instinctively looked past him at Jonathan's retreating form. He was still walking with Peter towards the lobby, deep in discussion, without a glance back.

"What are you doing here?" I hissed. "I told you—"

"People are beginning to stare, Mina. You have not given me a response," Abe replied, illustrating his point by extending his hand further.

I took a hasty look around. Several nearby guests were taking in our interaction with blatant interest. Across the room, Jane Newton was looking back and forth between me and Abe with narrowed eyes. I knew that I could not make a scene. Not here.

I grudgingly accepted his hand, allowing him to escort me to the dance floor. I stiffened as he pulled me close, once again acutely aware of his body so close to mine. We began to dance, and I forced a cordial smile for the sake of any curious onlookers.

"I don't know what you expect from me," I said in a low tone, still smiling. "If there is some sort of threat in London, let Scotland Yard handle it."

"You would not let me finish yesterday. The Ripper murders—it is not just prostitutes or even the poor who are being murdered or going missing." Abe's voice was as low as mine, a polite smile also pinned on his face, belying the urgency of his tone and the darkness of his words. "Upper-class men and women are being violently murdered as well, in neighborhoods like Mayfair and Saint James. Even in areas outside of London—Hertfordshire, Kent, Surrey. Over a dozen in the past month alone."

The smile froze on my face, and a chill spread through me as I stared at him with both horror and incredulity.

"Scotland Yard wants the public to believe the Ripper only targets prostitutes in Whitechapel. If the public knew that *respectable* people were being murdered as well, the panic would be immeasurable. The police worked with the press to sensationalize the prostitute murders to draw attention away from what was—is—happening."

"How do you know this?" I whispered.

"Inspector Seward, my friend and contact at Scotland Yard. Jack believes that there is more than one killer at large in London. I agree with him, but I do not think that they are human."

The music switched once again to a quadrille, but I remained rooted to the spot, my heart thundering wildly in my chest as I stared at Abe. He stepped forward, his lips close to my ear now, ensuring that I was the only one who could hear his next words.

"I believe that what happened to Arthur's wife and the Ripper murders are linked by the creature we encountered in Transylvania. I believe it is here in London."

5

CREATURES OF MYTH AND NIGHTMARE

As Abe's words sunk in, the memories of what I had seen in Transylvania flooded my mind's eye. The rumors of bodies drained of blood. The haunted faces of the villagers as they insisted that the *strigoi* walked among them. My father as he lay dead in that forest clearing, eyes permanently frozen wide in terror.

I took a faltering step back from Abe, shaking my head, as if to rid myself of the images. It could not be. Vampires were creatures of myth and nightmare; creatures who did not exist. *Could* not exist. The thought that they were real and here in London filled me with overwhelming terror.

Around us, the other guests had begun to dance the quadrille, casting us with curious looks. I could only imagine the gossip that would spread at the small scene Abe and I were making, but I found that I did not care. I took another step back from Abe, who was studying me with both concern and continued urgency.

"I–I need air," I stammered, turning to stumble blindly away through the crowd.

All sense of decorum forgotten, I pushed through the guests, ignoring their startled cries as I made my way off the crowded dance floor, weaving past the cluster of tables until I reached the rear balcony.

To my great relief it was empty, and I breathed in the refreshing, cool night air. I made my way to the rails of the balcony and leaned heavily against them. I heard Abe's footfalls behind me, and drew another wavering breath before turning around to face him.

He stopped several feet away. I could tell that he was desperate to continue, but he remained silent, waiting for me to speak.

"Why?" I asked. "If . . . if you believe this to be true, why would such creatures be here in London, targeting the upper-classes? Or the poor?"

"I do not know." Abe looked utterly baffled as he shook his head. "But I do know that similar murders and disappearances are happening in cities all around Europe—Paris, Berlin, Amsterdam. You are the only other person I know who's seen what I have seen. I have told Seward everything, and based on what he has seen, he believes me. But he would not dare bring up my theory to his colleagues. They would have us both committed."

"I still don't know how you expect me to help you. If vamp—if such creatures truly exist and are here in London, then I have no idea why. Surely, you've heard the rumors about my father? Even if I did come forward with what I saw in Transylvania, everyone would assume I've gone mad as well."

"You have more insight than you realize. At least speak to Jack and tell him what you saw. You do not have to detail what happened to your father, if that is what concerns you. He is already aware. You can help with—"

"No," I interrupted, fervently shaking my head. "I've already told you—I'm no longer a part of any of this and I can't help you. Please just leave me be."

I started to move past him to head back inside; but Abe stood firmly in my path.

"Abe, I insist that you—"

"Just answer me this one question, Mina," he interrupted. His voice had fallen flat, the desperation and urgency now gone. I studied him. His eyes were now blank, his expression guarded.

"Only if you give me your word that you will leave me be," I said, disconcerted by his sudden change of tone.

"You have it. I will not bother you again."

"All right," I said warily. "What is it?"

"Do you love him?"

It was such an abrupt change from what we'd been discussing that I was momentarily taken aback. Abe was no longer looking directly at me; instead, he was focused on some arbitrary point past my shoulder. I knew that he was trying to appear neutral, though he could not hide the vulnerability in his eyes.

"Yes," I replied, without hesitation. Even though I could still feel the traces of love I'd once harbored for Abe as I stood across from him now, I didn't doubt my love for Jonathan. With all that had happened the past few years, my feelings for him had become a stabilizing force that helped keep me out of the loop of constant grief that once plagued me. Yet a small stab of guilt pinched me at the admission, though there was no reason for it.

Abe nodded stiffly, his eyes betraying nothing. Still not looking at me, he took a step back, clearing the way for my exit.

I hesitated a moment before taking my leave, an odd sense of regret sweeping over me as I did so. I forced myself to keep walking without looking back, entering the ballroom to head back towards my seat.

My steps faltered when I saw Jonathan was already standing by my empty seat with a suspicious frown. His eyes shifted to look past me, and as

I turned, I saw Abe exiting the balcony as well, his head low as he moved towards the lobby.

I turned back towards Jonathan, anxious. How many society rules had I broken by spending time on the balcony alone with a man who was not my fiancé? Abe's words had so overwhelmed me that the rules of social propriety I had trained myself to follow had fallen away. The balcony was in clear view of where Jonathan now stood. Had he seen our heated exchange?

I reached Jonathan, opening my mouth to explain, but before I could speak, he took my arm and escorted me to the dance floor. The orchestra was playing another waltz, and he pulled me into his arms, his eyes settling on me without their usual warmth.

"Who was that?" he asked bluntly.

"Abraham Van Helsing. I've mentioned him. My—my father's former student," I replied, hating how guilty I sounded.

"The discussion seems to have upset you. What was it about?" he pressed, his tone edged with suspicion.

"He wants my help with something. Something from the past."

Jonathan stared at me for a disconcertingly long moment, as if trying to ascertain the truth of my words.

"Mina," he said finally, continuing to probe my

eyes with his. "Who exactly is Van Helsing to you? More than just your father's student, I assume?"

I faltered the steps of the waltz and nearly stumbled. Jonathan kept me steady, continuing to effortlessly swirl me around as he awaited my response.

I didn't want to discuss my romantic past with Abe here, but Jonathan's strained countenance demanded an immediate answer. I silently cursed myself for not telling him about Abe's reappearance last night, and Abe himself for showing up and unraveling the life I had slowly begun to put back together.

"He *was* Father's student," I replied. "But he was also . . . we were together. Before Father died. We were briefly engaged."

Jonathan expelled a sharp breath, but he didn't look as shocked as I thought he'd be. He must have already surmised the romantic nature of our relationship, and merely wanted me to confirm it.

"It was of little importance," I continued, trying to give him a reassuring smile. "It was years ago when I traveled with Father. I was so very young, and it never officially—"

"I'd already guessed. The way you two looked at each other on the balcony . . ." Jonathan said, his eyes shadowing. "I suppose I did not want to know," he added, trying to give me a wry smile, but it came off as pained instead.

"Jonathan, that relationship is in my past. You must know that."

"I do know," he conceded, softening as he gave me a gentle smile.

The waltz ended, and as Jonathan escorted me back to our seats, I relaxed. I had worried that Abe's appearance would ruin our evening, but Jonathan seemed calmer now.

Yet my ease was short-lived. Once we took our seats, Jonathan studied me for a long moment before he spoke.

"Forgive me my jealousy, but I must ask. Is this the first time you've seen Van Helsing?" he asked. "Since your engagement ended?"

I stiffened. Jonathan awaited my response, but I sensed that he already knew the answer. For a moment, I debated lying to him, but it was something my conscience wouldn't allow. I had already hidden too much from him. Once again, I cursed myself for not telling him of Abe's visit sooner.

"No," I replied, and Jonathan looked away from me. I tried to take his hand, but he pulled it out of my reach. "He came to see me yesterday after school. I assure you it's not what you're thinking. It—it's about the issue he wants my help with. Something that I don't want to be a part of."

"What does he want your help with?"

Jonathan was still not looking at me, instead staring straight ahead at the dance floor.

I clenched my hands in my lap. What would he

think of me if I told him of vampires? How could I possibly explain what had happened in Transylvania, when I could hardly understand it myself? He would think I was mad. I would lose him, and I could not lose him. I had suffered more than enough loss for a lifetime.

"It's difficult to explain," I stammered. Once again, I reached for his hand. To my relief, he didn't pull away. "Please, Jonathan. All of that is in the past. I won't be seeing him again. Let's try to enjoy the rest of our—"

"There is so much you haven't told me. We are to be wed, yet you keep so much of yourself hidden from me," Jonathan spat, finally turning to look at me, his hazel eyes filled with a mixture of hurt and anger. "I imagine your former fiancé knows more about you than I ever have," he added coldly.

"That's not true," I protested. Other guests were surreptitiously looking our way now. I drew a breath to calm myself, lowering my voice. "I prefer to leave my past behind me because it's painful . . . and it's no longer of any importance."

Jonathan got to his feet, forcing me to release my hand from his. When he looked down at me, his eyes were no longer filled with anger, only sadness.

"Have Stanley escort you back to Highgate. I'll take a cab."

"Jonathan, no. Let me come with you," I pleaded, stumbling to my feet.

Jonathan had already turned on his heel to

disappear into the swirling crowds of the ballroom. Desperate, I hurried after him, his name on my lips, when the ballroom suddenly plunged into darkness.

All around me, the guests' startled gasps and cries filled the ballroom. I halted, temporarily disoriented as my eyes adjusted to the sudden dark. I was certain that the lights would come back on shortly, but something felt wrong.

Dim moonlight filtered in through the windows, providing only faint illumination. I could now vaguely make out several tall figures moving through the disconcerted crowd. As I stood frozen to the spot, I felt a coldness on my skin—the same coldness I had felt at the cemetery when I'd sensed being watched.

I watched in horrified silence as the figures, who I could now tell were three men and one woman, moved through the ballroom so quickly that they seemed to vanish into thin air and reappear in a different place.

Dread stirred in the pit of my stomach as I recalled the words of the villagers in Transylvania. *The strigoi vanish and reappear. They move quickly. The darkness makes them strong.*

"No," I whispered.

It was impossible. It could not be.

I lurched forward, panic scorching through my veins like wildfire as I began to shove my way through the guests, who were all stumbling towards the exit. I felt the same instinct that struck me in the cemetery—to flee. I needed to find Jonathan and get as far away from the Langham as possible.

But as soon as I had the thought, the screams began.

6

THE VANISHING

Screams reverberated throughout the ballroom. All pretense of propriety cast aside, the guests around me pushed and shoved each other to get to the exit.

Panicked, I continued to force my way through the thick sea of bodies, searching desperately for any sign of Jonathan. I prayed that he had already left, but I was halfway across the ballroom when I spotted him on the far opposite side, next to one of the windows. He was standing stock still, staring in rapt attention at an unnaturally tall man and woman who stood opposite him.

"Jonathan!" I shouted. My cry echoed throughout the ballroom, louder than any of the screams that punctuated the chaos. Jonathan remained rooted to the spot, his focus centered on the two people before him. They both went still at my cry, turning to look at me.

I felt that familiar coldness settle over me as their gazes locked with mine. The man looked like an alabaster statue come to life, with hair as black as night, a long pale face, thin lips and full brows. The woman was as light as her companion dark, with a stark beauty that was almost unnatural. A curtain of long blonde waves framed her exquisitely carved features, and her vivid green eyes seemed to glow in the dim light.

Though I was certain I had never seen the man before, there was something oddly familiar about him, and I thought I saw a brief glimpse of recognition flare in his black eyes as they settled on me. They both turned back to face Jonathan, who still stood motionless, as if he were in a trance. Their lips moved as they spoke to him in low tones, and my body went rigid with shock when I saw . . . fangs. Fangs protruding from their rows of angular teeth.

I had seen such fangs before, on the creature that hovered over Father's body that night, sharpened fangs that seemed to glint in the moonlight. I had convinced myself that it was a trick of the light; I had not seen them clearly, I had been in terrible shock—anything to explain away what I'd actually seen.

But standing here now, I could not deny the sight of them. And I knew with a sudden and terrifying certainty that they were creatures I had refused to believe existed . . . did not want to believe existed.

The intruders were vampires.

The creature we encountered in Transylvania. I believe it is here in London, Abe had whispered, only moments before.

Fear propelled me out of my shocked stillness, and I stumbled forward, my heart pounding so powerfully that it seemed to rattle my bones. I didn't know why they were here, I just had to get Jonathan away from them.

As I shoved through the crowd, I saw the vampires step closer to my transfixed fiancé, almost seeming to wrap themselves around him, until he was hidden from my view.

"*JONATHAN!*" I screamed.

I was now only ten yards away from them, but it seemed as if there were a vast ocean between us, and the fleeing guests continued to impede my forward progress.

The male vampire turned to give me a look that gleamed with challenge, and I watched with dazed horror as the vampires and Jonathan *vanished* before my eyes. The space where they'd just stood was now empty.

I froze, unable to believe what I had just seen. The vanishing was another echo of that gruesome night in Transylvania. I scanned the area near the window and the entire ballroom for any sign of

Jonathan and the vampires as the guests around me continued to scramble out of the emptying ballroom. In the chaos, no one else seemed to notice Jonathan and the vampires' disappearance.

The ballroom lights flickered back on, flooding the room with glaring light. I stumbled forward, reaching the spot where Jonathan had just stood. I whirled, searching the ballroom for any sign of him, but only a few stupefied guests remained.

I turned to search the streets outside the window, now dense with a heavy fog. Amidst the cluster of carriages in front of the Langham, I noticed two distinct black landau carriages—larger and finer in appearance than even the most grandiose upper-class London carriage—made of wrought iron and edged with gold trim.

The fog partially cleared, and I saw that velvet curtains were drawn over the glass windows of both carriages, but the left door of one was slightly open. Jonathan sat inside with several other women I did not recognize, looking dazed and out of sorts.

I felt a burst of hope at the sight of him. As if sensing my gaze, Jonathan looked up and met my eyes, blinking in disorientation. Before I could cry out to him, some invisible force slammed the door shut, and both carriages sped away.

"Mina!"

I turned and saw Abe hurrying towards me, his face pale with relief. Shaking, I stepped forward to grip his shoulders.

"Jonathan's been abducted—he's in a carriage that just left. Do you have a horse?"

I was thankful that he didn't question me. He grabbed my hand, leading me towards the rear exit of the ballroom.

"I took a cab here, but there are horses in the stable yard at the back," he said. "Come."

We broke into a run, dashing through the now empty ballroom towards the exit. Though a multitude of panicked questions raced through my mind over what I'd just witnessed, I kept them at bay. I needed to focus on getting Jonathan back while there was still time; my questions could be answered later.

In the rear of the Langham, we found unattended horses tethered in the stable yard. Their masters had no doubt heard the ruckus and ran inside to see what was happening.

We untethered two horses and mounted them to race out of the stable yard.

"It was two landau carriages—they went down Regent Street!" I shouted to Abe, gripping the reins of my horse.

As we rode away from the Langham and towards Regent Street, the crisp night air pricked at my skin, and the damp wispy fog swirled around us like thin ghostly fingers. At this late hour, there weren't many carriages out, and the distinctive black carriage that had taken Jonathan away was nowhere in sight. We were silent as we raced down the fog-encased street towards Whitehall, and it was only the sound of my thundering heartbeat, our horses' hooves pounding on the ground, and the murmur of voices from startled passersby that accompanied us.

Abe rode at my side, his eyes trained on the street ahead. The rigid set of his shoulders was the only indication of his tension. My knuckles were white from gripping the reins in my trembling hands, and a haze of panic clouded my mind. I could only hope we were going in the right direction.

Regent Street soon turned into Whitehall, and hope seared my chest as I spotted the distinct black carriages only fifty yards ahead, clamoring forward at a great speed.

"There they are!" I cried, kicking the sides of my horse to urge him into a faster gallop, and I soon left Abe behind.

I'm right behind you, Jonathan, I thought desperately, keeping my eyes trained on the carriages as I sped forward.

The carriages turned onto Westminster Bridge, and I followed suit. The gothic spires of Westminster rose from the fog that surrounded the bridge, a silent spectator to my chase. I was getting closer to the carriages now, swiftly closing the gap between us.

But just as the carriages reached the midway

point of the bridge, they were swallowed up by an even thicker fog that seemed to rise up out of nowhere, as if it had been conjured, and I could no longer make them out.

I stilled with horror as a deeply rich male voice rose from the silence, wrapping around me in a dark whisper.

"Ghyslaine . . . what you have tried to destroy will be made whole once more."

I halted at the strange words, pulling back on the reins. My horse reared back in surprise, neighing in protest and nearly throwing me from the saddle. I managed to maintain my grip on the reins as I looked around in despair. The voice had seemed to come from everywhere and nowhere, yet I was completely alone on the bridge. As the thick fog dissipated, the two black carriages were nowhere to be seen.

They had vanished . . . along with Jonathan.

"There were four of them, I believe. And the carriages appeared aristocratic. They didn't look like the others that were gathered," I said, desperate.

I was back in the ballroom of the Langham, standing opposite an incredulous looking inspector from Scotland Yard. When Abe had caught up to me on Westminster Bridge, I was staring off in a numb daze at the foggy horizon where the carriage had vanished, and I had not protested when he told me that we should return to the Langham.

We made our way back in silence, the night's events swirling about in my mind. The vampires seeming to wrap themselves around Jonathan, the male vampire's cold gaze on me in the darkness, the black carriages vanishing in the fog, the whispered voice on the bridge. I hadn't told Abe about the voice I heard on the bridge. I wasn't even sure it had been a voice, or if I'd gone temporarily mad from all that had occurred.

When we arrived back at the Langham, the guests who remained had spilled out onto the streets outside of the hotel, murmuring heatedly amongst themselves. Curious onlookers now surrounded the building, clogging the narrow streets. Several Scotland Yard inspectors and police officers had arrived, and were taking formal reports and interviewing witnesses about the electrical outage and the chaos that followed. After we returned our horses to their incensed masters with hasty apologies, we approached one of the inspectors.

I was now trying to explain what had happened to Jonathan, careful to omit the less believable parts of my story. But the inspector still studied me with abject disbelief, his eyes periodically straying to Abe, as if for verification. But Abe remained oddly and infuriatingly silent.

"You are saying these carriages headed across Westminster Bridge," the inspector said.

"Yes," I said. "I–I couldn't keep track of them once they crossed. But they may still be in London, if—"

"There are, at any time in London, thousands of carriages on the street, Miss Murray," the inspector said. "None of the waiting carriage drivers saw anything out of the ordinary."

"Well, *I* saw something out of the ordinary," I snapped, blinking back tears of frustration. "And now my fiancé is missing. What are you—"

"Miss Murray, you are being hysterical. There was a malfunction with the electricity and many were separated in the chaos. We are currently conducting a search for guests who are unaccounted for, including your fiancé. If we do not locate Mister Harker—"

"You won't locate him, because he's been taken!" I cried. I turned to Abe. "Abe, please. Tell him."

"Mina," Abe said gently, addressing me but giving the inspector an apologetic smile. "It has been a long night. It will not help Jonathan at all if you drive yourself mad with worry. Now, I am certain that he is at a nearby tavern. Let me escort you home. Thank you for your time, Inspector."

I glared at him in angry disbelief as the inspector tipped his hat, giving me a condescending smile before walking away.

"Why did you do that?" I asked in furious disbelief. "You were practically mute. You saw everything that happened tonight. You were the one who—"

"He was not going to believe you no matter what you said. I needed you to see that for yourself. We cannot rely on the authorities. Jack is the only policeman who will believe you." He studied me intently before lowering his voice. "Am I correct in my assumption that you do accept what we are dealing with?"

He did not need to say the word 'vampire' for me to know what he was referring to. I closed my eyes, thinking of the incredulity in the inspector's eyes as I told him what happened to Jonathan. It was as familiar to me as the incredulity in the eyes of the authorities in Transylvania when I'd desperately tried to explain how Father died. I could only imagine what he would have said if I told him all that I'd actually seen tonight.

Abe was right. We could not rely on the authorities. We were on our own. Perhaps a part of me had known all along that Abe was right about vampires existing and being here in London. I had desperately wanted it not to be true, for it would force me to accept other horrible truths. But it was like a veil had been lifted, and I could not deny what I had seen tonight, nor in that forest in Transylvania three years ago. Not anymore.

A sudden wave of determination pulled me

from the horrified daze I'd been in since watching Jonathan vanish before my eyes. I would not lose him as I had lost my father, nor envelop myself in denial as I'd done for the last three years. I would do whatever it took to save him.

When I opened my eyes, I said, "I'm going after Jonathan. I must."

"Then you need to come with me," Abe said, not at all surprised by my statement as he extended his hand. "Let me help you. I believe I have a way of finding out where he is."

I took Abe's hand, and together we hurried out of the ballroom.

7

LUCY

Heavy sheets of rain fell from the sky as Abe and I raced past the fleeing villagers towards the forest that lay at the village's edge. Gripping my kukri, I scanned the trees around us as we entered the forest, shouting for my father.

I froze when I heard an agonized cry from the depths of the forest ahead. It was his voice. I had never heard such a sound from him.

No, I thought in agony. No.

We dashed forward, the muddy forest floor slowing our progress. I continued to search our surroundings for any sign of my father, my voice raw with trepidation as I continued to shout for him.

And then . . . I saw it. I stopped in my tracks, a tidal wave of horror rising in my stomach at the sight before me.

In a clearing yards ahead, there was a figure

hunched over the prostrated form of my father. At this distance, and from the way the figure was crouched, I could not tell whether it was man or beast.

I started to scramble forward, but a sudden paralysis settled over me, and I could not move. At my side, Abe was frozen in place as well. I struggled to release myself from the mysterious paralysis that held me, but its force was too great.

The figure turned and in the darkness and rain, I could only make out a flash of unnaturally long and sharp teeth and the feel of a frosty stare on my skin.

With an unnatural hiss, the creature vanished, and I was free of the paralysis. I rushed forward, filled with panic and dread, Father's name on my lips in a desperate cry.

I stumbled to my knees when I reached his still form. A pool of blood drenched the mud around his body, and his lifeless eyes, forever frozen wide, stared at me from what remained of his face. An agonized moan swelled from some place deep, and it emerged from my lips in a grief stricken scream.

"Mina?"

I blinked, forced out of the dark memory by Abe's voice. I was seated next to Abe in the back of a cab, and he was looking at me with a worried frown.

Abe had informed me that we were going to the home of Arthur Holmwood, the friend who summoned him to London. Inspector Seward was already there. We had not spoken as the cab rattled through the streets, and that was when the long-buried memory of Father's death sprang to life.

I looked past Abe out the window. The cab had arrived at a large Mayfair town home. I gave Abe a brief nod to indicate that I was all right, and we stepped out. Abe didn't inquire about my thoughts as we approached the front door of Arthur's home, though I could feel his fretful scrutiny of my expression.

Moments later, I stood in Arthur's spacious drawing room, opposite Inspector Jack Seward. Seward had hair the color of burnished copper and brown eyes that were shadowed with fatigue. Even though he wore no uniform, he had the look of a policeman—an inherent inquisitiveness paired with wary suspicion seemed to be his default expression. His hair was haphazardly spiked, as if he had repeatedly raked his hand through it, and he was pacing the room when we entered. He looked startled to see me, taking in my ball gown, and gave me a nod when Abe introduced us.

"Miss Murray," he said politely, before his questioning gaze slid to Abe. "You convinced her?"

Abe quickly filled him in on the events of the evening. When he was finished, Seward sank down into an armchair, burying his face in his hands. When he finally looked up, his face was ashen.

"Bloody hell," he whispered. He flushed,

looking at me and muttering a hasty apology before returning his attention to Abe. "On the night that I'm not on duty. How many were taken?"

"It is my hope that you can find that out from your colleagues. If we know exactly who else besides Jonathan was taken, then we could perhaps deduce why they were taken—process of elimination, anything they had in common—perhaps even some sort of connection. But for the present, I am going to speak with Lucy."

"Lucy?" Seward breathed. "She can't—"

"Mina, please follow me," Abe interrupted, ignoring Seward.

Seward's mouth tightened, but he fell silent. Abe left the drawing room, gesturing for me to follow.

He led me and an uncertain Seward down the long hallway outside the drawing room to a door, which I assumed led to the cellar. Abe swung open the door, reaching for a lantern that rested by the entrance before descending down the stairs. The lantern only provided slight illumination for the pitch-black cellar, and a shiver of unease went through me as we entered. As my eyes struggled to adjust to the dark, I heard a soft voice.

"Abraham?"

A man stepped out from the shadows, holding up a lantern of his own. He had blonde hair and pale blue eyes that blinked at Abe from behind a pair of spectacles. He barely seemed to notice mine and Seward's presence, his attention focused entirely on Abe.

"Has there been any change, Arthur?" Abe queried, stepping forward.

"It has gotten worse, if possible," Arthur replied, his voice quavering. Abe stepped forward to rest his hand on Arthur's shoulder.

"I am sorry, you know I am. But something has happened at the Langham. The creatures that did this to her have abducted several people, including my friend's fiancé," he said, gesturing to me. Arthur's eyes found mine in the soft light of the lantern, and I saw a faint glimmer of sympathy in his eyes. "I need to speak to Lucy—to try to communicate with the one who did this to her."

I looked back and forth between them, my confusion growing. Abe wanted to communicate *through* Lucy?

Arthur gave his consent with a mere jerk of his head. Abe turned to me, as if sensing my unasked question, and gestured for me to follow him further into the cellar. Arthur hung behind as Seward and I continued forward, trailing Abe towards a human-sized cage in the far rear of the cellar.

I halted at the sight of it, panic skittering through me as inhuman growls erupted from the cage. Abe lifted his lantern, illuminating what was inside, and my heart nearly stopped at the sight.

An eerily pale woman was crouched inside, her talon-like fingers wrapped around the cage bars.

Her thin, papery skin was pulled taut over her bones, and the eyes that peered at us beneath a curtain of long stringy brown hair seemed to shift from a deep brown to an unnatural black. She emitted another growl, and I saw that her two front incisors were elongated into . . . fangs.

My hand flew to my mouth to stifle a cry.

"She is still human, but in the midst of a transformative process. A fortnight ago, she and Arthur got into a terrible row. She left and went missing for two days. Arthur searched for her to no avail. When she returned home, she was different."

"Different how?" I whispered.

"At first . . . she did not speak," Arthur's strained voice replied, from behind me. I turned to face him as he approached. His eyes were haunted, trained on Lucy as he spoke.

"She was dangerously pale. Her eyes were no longer her own. They would shift in color from brown to black. She did not speak for hours, and when she did, it was in growls. She did not remember where she had been, or what had happened to her. She would only speak to tell me how thirsty she was. I took her to the doctor, but she . . . she attacked him. She almost gauged out his throat. I had to beg the doctor to keep his silence. I knew the police would take her to an institution if he reported her. I brought her back home and hid her away. I did not know what was happening to her—only that it was unnatural."

A chill swept over me as Arthur spoke, and I briefly met Abe's eyes. We had heard similar stories in the Transylvanian countryside.

"It is my belief that a vampire did this to her," Abe said, turning to face me. "I am still uncertain as to how the transformation process works. From lore it begins with a bite, and Lucy has two puncture wounds on the side of her neck—similar to wounds on the bodies drained of blood that Jack has found during his murder investigations. I do not know how many vampires are in London, but something tells me that they are working together—I will explain why later. If that is so, the vampire who bit Lucy may have some connection to the abductions at the Langham. I want to attempt to communicate with it."

Now I understood Seward's incredulity. I stared at him with disbelief of my own.

"How?" I breathed.

"Just keep your eyes on me. I need everyone to stay back."

After a moment of hesitation, I took a step back, along with Seward. Arthur remained where he was, his sad eyes trained on the creature that had been his wife. Abe gave him a long look, and Arthur responded with a nod.

Abe stepped towards the cage, kneeling down opposite her. I felt a strong urgency to warn him as her black eyes settled on him. Abe took out a silver locket from his pocket; it glinted in the dimness of the cellar as he held it up before her. Her gaze slid from his face to the locket, suddenly transfixed. She went very still, her ragged breathing slowing to a calm and steady rhythm. He was hypnotizing her.

"Who are you?" Abe asked her, his voice very gentle now, as if he were speaking to a small child.

"No one," Lucy replied, her voice throatily seductive for such a frail and wild looking woman, her eyes still trained on the locket. "Every one."

"Your kind came to the ballroom at the Langham Hotel tonight," Abe continued, undeterred by her cryptic response. "There were four of you. You took people, including a man named Jonathan Harker. Why? Where are you taking him?"

I stiffened, a sliver of hope emerging from beneath my shock. Could it be possible? Could he somehow communicate with the vampire who took Jonathan . . . through Lucy?

Lucy expelled a long sigh, her eyes distant as she continued to focus on the locket. She didn't respond, and Abe spoke again, his tone sharper this time.

"Where are you taking him?"

Lucy's eyes left the locket, rising to meet his, and I let out a soft gasp as the whites of her eyes went completely black. But Abe did not flinch.

"We need them," she said softly in reply.

I pressed my hands to my mouth to prevent myself from crying out. I wanted to lurch forward and shake her, to get more answers, but I forced myself to remain still.

"Why?" Abe demanded. "Where are you taking them?"

"One of the old safe places," she murmured, and a fond smile touched her lips. "Our old home in the Carpathians. A fortress impossible to enter."

"The Carpathians?" Abe echoed. "Transylvania? Is that where you are taking him? *Why him?*"

But Lucy fell silent once more, her eyes glazing over as she stared past Abe's shoulder at nothing.

I was no longer able to hold myself back. If she somehow knew where Jonathan was, I had to find out. I stumbled forward, kneeling down in front of the cage so that I was at her level, wrapping my hands around the bars. I could feel Abe go rigid at my side, but I no longer felt fear as she turned her focus towards me—only desperation.

"Where is Jonathan?" I demanded, desperate. "Tell me where—"

With a ferocious hiss, Lucy lunged at the bars, her fangs bared. Abe yanked me back just as the tips of her fangs pierced the delicate skin of my left forefinger. I stumbled back, clutching my bleeding finger, watching in disgust as she eagerly licked up the remnants of my blood from her lips.

As her black eyes met mine, I saw a brief flicker of recognition, similar to the one I had seen from the male vampire at the ball. But her eyes suddenly went hazy and unfocused. She curled up on the floor of the cage, wrapping her arms around herself, trembling violently, as if she were having a seizure.

Arthur, who had completely frozen during her outburst, came to life and raced towards the cage. He kneeled down, looking both panicked and hopeful.

"Lucy!" he shouted. "Lucy, my angel, are you back? Is that you?"

She slowly looked up, her eyes wide and frightened, their color now a natural brown. She looked scared, vulnerable, and . . . human.

"Arthur?" she whispered.

8

TRANSYLVANIA

"How did you do that?" I asked Abe, thoroughly shaken.

We were now gathered in Arthur's large but cramped study. Abe had administered the confused and increasingly frantic Lucy a sedative, while Arthur wrapped her in blankets before reluctantly locking the cage door and leading us out of the cellar.

I stood opposite Abe, rattled by what I had seen him do. Arthur had just left the room to bring us tea, while Seward quietly stood in front of the fireplace, his eyes troubled as he gazed into its leaping flames.

"After your father's death, I started researching vampires when I returned to Amsterdam—as mad as it seemed—but I could not forget what we had seen. I needed to make sense of it. I began to analyze all of the notes we had taken from our travels in the region, including Robert's. It was his theory that if vampires did indeed exist, they exhibited traits that were similar to wolves. As Darwin theorized that man is related to ape, Robert theorized that vampires may be related to wolves. I certainly could not experiment on an actual vampire, so I experimented on their potential relatives—wolves. In my experiments, I observed that silver has a calming effect on wolves, and it has a medicinal effect on humans. For vampires, I deduced that it would have a combined effect and potentially work as a hypnotic. When Arthur first had me examine Lucy, my silver locket instantly calmed her, and I was able to put her under hypnosis."

I studied him, guilt battling with my awe at his experimentation. I had always admired Abe's quiet brilliance, his ability to think in ways that most people did not.

But my guilt outweighed my awe. While Abe had spent the past three years trying to reconcile what we had seen in Transylvania, I had been in abject denial; trying to push it all away as if it had never happened.

"You were able to *speak* with one of those bloody vamp . . . those things through Lucy," Seward said, aghast, as he turned to face Abe. "How's that possible?"

"Wolves are pack animals. Pack animals have sophisticated methods of non-verbal communication—I just took it further. As vampires are outside of nature, I theorized that they must also have preternatural ways of communication, and the conclusion that I came to—"

"Telepathic communication," I whispered, as I recalled the voice that seemed to wrap around me on Westminster Bridge.

"Yes," Abe said, looking surprised at my completion of his thought. "It explains how they are able to coordinate such quick and strategic attacks, often in groups, like we just saw in the Langham—and as witnesses described in Transylvania. I did not know if *communication* through hypnosis would work on Lucy, until I tried it just now."

Abe's face was mildly unsettled as he took a seat in one of the chairs; his calm during his interaction with Lucy had been a facade. He was just as astonished as we were that he could communicate through her.

Arthur entered with a tray of tea, apologetically explaining that he had dismissed the servants to dissuade gossip when Lucy first began acting strangely. I accepted a cup with a polite nod, deciding that there would be no better time than now to tell them what had happened on Westminster Bridge.

"When I was chasing after the carriage on Westminster Bridge, I heard a voice. I believe it was the voice of the vampire who took Jonathan," I said, after a brief moment of hesitation. "At first I thought I was going mad. But if you're right, Abe, and they're able to communicate through telepathy—"

"What did he say?" Abe interrupted, his voice strained with tension. Seward and Arthur were also regarding me with anxious eyes.

I took a breath before repeating the chilling words that were now burned into my memory.

"Ghyslaine . . . what you have tried to destroy will be made whole once more."

Stunned silence met my words. Arthur and Seward exchanged baffled looks, while Abe's brow furrowed with worry.

"Ghyslaine. What's that?" Seward finally asked.

"I don't know, but right before he took Jonathan, he looked at me with . . . recognition. As if he knew who I was. I don't know how that's possible."

Abe rubbed at his temples, a gesture I recognized. He did this whenever he was deep in thought, attempting to come up with a solution to a complex problem.

"If what Lucy told us is correct, we know where they're taking Jonathan," I said. I needed to return the focus to Jonathan. "The Carpathian Mountains in Transylvania. That is where we must go."

"Wait," Seward protested, turning to Abe.

"How do you know you were talking with the same creature who took Jonathan? Or that she was even talking about Transylvania? Aren't the Carpathians massive? Lucy could've just been—"

"We don't. But Transylvania is the most likely explanation," I interrupted, before Abe could respond. "My father was killed in a Transylvanian village not far from the Carpathians, and Transylvania is where we recorded multiple witness accounts of vampires."

"You're suggesting that we just go to some fortress in Transylvania—of which there are many—to face creatures we know nothing about?" Seward demanded in disbelief.

While Seward was right to be hesitant and cautious, I knew we had no choice. I was determined to rescue Jonathan regardless of the danger and the odds against us, and I felt an unnerving certainty that if I didn't go after him he would be lost forever.

"We can gather reinforcements," I said desperately, thinking aloud. "When we last traveled through the region, we came across villagers who lost many of their own to vampire attacks. At the time, we thought they were just being superstitious, and the deaths were caused by illness or some other rational cause. But now we know better. Surely they'll be willing to help us."

"You still don't know what we're up against. An army of angry villagers against those things is not

—" Seward began, frustrated. He turned to Abe, as if appealing to him for reason. "Abe, I know I've been hesitant in involving my colleagues at Scotland Yard, but maybe now we should—"

"You know better than anyone that we can't go to the police," I protested, my desperation rising. "The inspector I spoke to tonight thought I was mad—and I didn't even tell him what I actually saw! How do you think your colleagues will react when we inform them that mythical creatures abducted my fiancé from the Langham?"

"Mina is right," Abe said. "Your memory seems to fail you, Jack. They nearly sacked you when you first broached the possibility of the Ripper not being human—that is why you sent for me."

"When I proposed to the doctor that what happened to Lucy is wholly unnatural," Arthur spoke up, his voice tinged with anger. "He nearly contacted the authorities to report me. I had to assure him my grief made me unable to think rationally."

"Then we are in agreement about the authorities," I said, turning back towards Seward, who still looked uncertain. "Inspector Seward, you are under no obligation to come with us, but I am going to rescue my fiancé and bring him home. Mister Holmwood, do you have maps of the region?"

"Yes. Please, call me Arthur. I believe that referring to each other by our Christian names is appropriate, given the circumstances," Arthur replied, brushing past Seward to open one of the cabinets that lined the study. Seward remained rigid, but offered no further protest as Arthur flipped through several rolled up maps before withdrawing one and bringing it to his desk, where he spread it out.

Abe and I stepped forward to examine it. The map showed Transylvania and the neighboring region of Wallachia to the south.

"This is from a surveyor friend of mine. He has been to Eastern Europe many times. Do you see there?" he asked, pointing to various triangle shaped marks on the map. "He highlighted old castles and fortresses in the region." He tapped one particular marked spot located at the base of the Carpathian Mountain range. "This is the only fortress in this region of the mountains. It could very well be the fortress Lucy referred to."

Dread mingled with hope as I centered my gaze on the base of the mountains in the northern part of Transylvania. The area was indeed mere kilometers from the village where Father had been killed.

"Arthur," Abe said suddenly, looking up at his friend. "I know this may seem like a cruel and impossible demand," he added, speaking very carefully, as if he expected an explosive response to his words. "But I think we should bring Lucy with us."

Seward, Arthur and I stared at him in quiet disbelief.

"Why?" I asked. "She's in no state to—"

"Lucy was possibly able to determine where they are taking Jonathan," Abe said, addressing me but looking at Arthur. "We may be able to keep track of where these creatures are through her."

"Dear God, Abraham," Arthur breathed, looking ill as he stumbled back from the desk. "My wife may be afflicted with something monstrous, but she is still a human being! I will not let you use her as a compass. I have helped you thus far because you are a friend and for what you have done for us, but do not try my patience."

Abe fell silent, and I could see a shadow of guilt in his eyes as he looked away, giving Arthur a curt nod. I sensed that had not been easy for him to ask.

But Abe was right. Lucy could help us greatly.

"Arthur," I said, hesitant. "I–I think that Abe is right. Think of it . . . Lucy may be our only way of tracking these creatures down to destroy them. You know your wife. If she were lucid, would she want to do this? Would she be willing to help us?"

Arthur lowered his gaze, taking off his spectacles to rub his eyes, which were stormy with conflict. He moved towards the fireplace, gazing down into the flames for several long moments before turning back to face me.

"God help me," he breathed, and his eyes now shining with tears. "My Lucy is a kind soul, and she would want to help. I–I suppose I have no choice but to give you my consent," he whispered. "But I am coming with you as well. When we find the creature who did this to her . . . I am going to kill him."

"Jack?" Abe asked quietly, turning to Seward, who still hovered silently in the corner of the room. "Are you with us? I will understand if you wish to remain in London."

"I still think this plan's damned foolhardy," Seward said, raking a hand through his hair as he gave me an apologetic look for the oath. "But anyone outside of this room would think I'm mad—that we're all mad fools. I've seen firsthand what these monsters have done to the innocent. I can no longer stand idly by while more are killed."

The silence that followed was heavy; rife with the acknowledgement of the treacherous journey that lie ahead of us. I was not one to believe in destiny or fate, Father had always insisted that it was our choices that determined our path in life. But it seemed now as if my return to Transylvania was somehow predetermined; the path I had taken to escape what I'd seen that horrible night had ultimately become cyclical, leading me right back and forcing me to confront the monster that dwelt there.

"Well," I said, evenly meeting their eyes. "Let's all be mad fools together, shall we?"

9

THE PROMISE

Before leaving the Holmwood residence, we made hasty plans for our departure from England. The next train from Charing Cross to Dover, from which we would take a ferry to Calais, left in the late morning. Arthur was well acquainted with the captain of a cargo ship that was departing earlier from Tilbury Docks with a stop in Calais before continuing on to a port in Varna.

"The accommodations will be rather rough, but it would get us to Calais sooner," Arthur said apologetically, looking at me.

"I don't care about the state of our accommodations. I just want to get there as soon as possible," I said, bristling at his focus on me, the sole woman in the room. I had traveled in plenty of ragged conditions with Father, and I never cared about luxury during travel. Especially under these circumstances.

"From Calais, we will take a train to Paris and board the Orient Express to Budapest. We can then transfer to Klausenburgh, in Transylvania," Arthur continued. "We can disembark there and arrange for horses to travel the rest of the way."

"That will take us through the countryside. We can gather potential reinforcements from the villages we ride through." Abe added.

"I will send a wire to arrange for our tickets. Barring any delays, we can arrive the day after tomorrow," Arthur said.

I nodded, hoping that would be enough time to get to Jonathan before any harm came to him. *Unless it's already too late*, a dark thought whispered in my mind.

We then reviewed what weapons we already possessed. I had my kukri knives, Seward had a revolver, and Abe had an assortment of knives that he could share with us if it became necessary.

"I have a sword cane," Arthur said hesitantly.

I looked at Arthur in surprise. He was every inch the London gentleman; I could hardly imagine him fighting anyone. From the looks on their faces, Abe and Seward shared my sentiment.

"It has been in my family for generations. My father insisted that Holmwood men be armed at all times. I once took lessons from a top fencing master," Arthur continued, with a trace of defensiveness at our obvious surprise.

"We should be settled with weapons for now. If we need more, I have contacts along the route we are traveling," Abe said, giving Arthur a quick nod. "But we will need more specialized weapons if we encounter more than one of those creatures along the way."

Though I knew what we were facing, apprehension still pierced me at his words. Would I be prepared to fight one of those creatures? Even with my self-defense training, I didn't feel confident in my abilities. But I had no choice. I would do what was necessary to rescue Jonathan.

We filed out of Arthur's study after agreeing to meet at the entrance to the Tilbury Docks the next morning. While Seward headed to his home in Stratford, Abe left with me to collect some of my father's journals and records from his office that could potentially be useful during our journey. He didn't need to pack—the one bag he'd brought with him from Amsterdam had barely been touched.

As we traveled towards Highgate, unanswered questions swam through my mind. Why had Jonathan been taken? Who was that strange vampire who seemed to recognize me, and what did his words on Westminster Bridge mean? Why were vampires here in London? How many were there?

By the time we arrived at my home, I was

quaking with anxiety, and Abe reached out to give my arm a comforting squeeze.

"It will do you no good to worry," he said. "We will get him back. You need to remain focused."

I nodded, trying to heed his words. We approached my front door, which swung open to reveal a worried Clara standing in the entrance hall.

"Mina! T'ank heavens. Where've you been?! I've been—" she began, sounding both angry and relieved. Her eyes fell on Abe and she fell silent, her countenance shifting from one of chastisement to confusion.

"Abraham?" she breathed, blinking at him in surprise. "What're you—"

"Jonathan's been abducted," I interrupted, pushing past her to step inside.

My intention had been to quickly explain what happened so that we could be on our way, but saying the words aloud broke something within me, and a sudden rush of tears sprang to my eyes. Clara gasped, pulling me into the soothing warmth of her arms. The emotional barrier I had carefully erected to maintain my stoicism collapsed, and I began to weep.

"Oh, Mina," she whispered, gently stroking my hair.

My fears for Jonathan and the journey that lay ahead came out through my tears, and I wept for several long moments as Clara rocked me in her arms.

When my tears subsided, I pulled back, wiping my eyes. Both Clara and Abe had seen me cry before, but I was still embarrassed by my outpouring of emotion. *Focus on getting Jonathan back*, I reminded myself. *Tears will accomplish nothing*.

"I–I will explain as much as I can, but we must hurry. I need help packing, and Abe needs access to Father's study," I said, taking a calming breath as I blinked back the remainder of my tears.

"Packin'?" Clara asked, an undercurrent of panic in her voice.

"We believe we know where he is, and we're going after him. We leave at first light." I replied, in a tone that did not welcome argument.

"If Jonathan's been abducted, can't t' police handle it?" Clara persisted.

"Jonathan's abductor is not human, I am afraid," Abe said bluntly. "The police cannot help us."

Clara's hands flew to her mouth and her eyes went wide. I gave Abe a sharp look for his plainness, reaching out to gently grasp Clara's arm.

"I'll explain everything while I pack," I repeated, my tone softer this time, but maintaining its urgency. "Please give Abe access to Father's study. We need some of his records." My despair of just moments earlier had shifted back to determination, and I moved toward the stairs without waiting for her reply.

Efficient as always, Clara managed to put her astonishment aside. She gave Abe access to Father's study, made us both tea, and helped me put together a traveling bag. As I started to give her the full details of the night's events, a knock sounded at the door.

Both Clara and I froze. I dropped the cloak I was holding and whirled towards the doorway of my bedroom, an impossible hope swelling in my chest. Could it be Jonathan? Was he still here in London—safe? Who else would be calling at this late hour?

I ran out of my room, flying down the hallway past a stunned Abe, who had appeared at the doorway of Father's study at the sound of the knock. I could feel his and Clara's eyes on me as I raced down the stairs, tore across the entrance hall, and flung open the door.

My hope deflated when I saw who stood there.

"Where is my son?" Mary Harker snapped, glaring at me with barely suppressed rage as she pushed past me to step into the entrance hall.

I closed the door, turning to face her. Before Abe and I had left the Langham, I'd informed the Harker carriage driver to deliver a message to Mary with a revised version of the night's events—only mentioning the electrical outage and that Jonathan and I had been separated amidst the chaos. I made sure the message noted that I was in contact with Scotland Yard only as a precaution, as I was certain that I would locate Jonathan shortly. It was a blatant lie, but I did not have the time to deal with Mary's outrage and hysteria.

"Did you receive my message?" I asked with stiff politeness, trying to maintain my calm.

"You mean your casual note about my only child disappearing?" Mary hissed. "Yes, I did. I immediately went to the Langham and then Scotland Yard to make my own report. Jane Newton was still at the Langham when I arrived. She told me everyone saw you and Jonathan having a row. You were dallying with another man and my son was reasonably upset," Mary seethed, her outrage growing with every word. "He stormed off because you broke his heart."

"That's not true," I said hastily, though she was not far from the truth. I silently cursed Jane Newton for her meddling. "I don't know where Jonathan is, but—"

"We are looking for him," Abe finished my sentence, entering the hall behind me.

I closed my eyes. I had been so focused on Mary that I didn't hear him come down the stairs. He was only going to make things worse. Indeed, Mary's eyes went so wide at his presence that it would have been comical under different circumstances.

"And just who are you?" she spat.

"Abraham Van Helsing. I was a colleague of Mina's late father," Abe replied, unperturbed by Mary's outrage.

"I . . . heavens, if you are spending the night—" Mary sputtered, looking back and forth between us, her indignation growing. "For an engaged woman to have another man lodge with her! That is most—"

"He's not lodging here, Mary," I said, taking a deep breath in an effort to keep my tone steady. "He's helping me look for Jonathan. We—"

"This . . . this is an outrage!" Mary shouted, as if I had not spoken at all. She turned her furious gaze back towards me. "I never understood what my son saw in you. You have no breeding and you are not a proper lady. When he returns, I will make it my priority to end your engagement. He will happily end it himself when I report what I have witnessed here," she continued, looking at me and Abe in disgust, as if she had caught us *in flagrante delicto*.

I glared at her, my resolve to maintain calm rapidly failing. With all of the events of the evening, the usual politeness I wore like a shield around Mary fell away.

"I am not a lady," I snapped.

"I beg your pardon?" Her tone was filled with disbelief.

"I am not a lady, and that is why Jonathan loves me. That is why I will find him, and that is why I insist that you leave my home immediately, or I will not be responsible for the consequences!"

Mary stumbled back, her hand flying towards her chest. I noted with pleasure that she looked a bit frightened, and she was trying unsuccessfully to hide it. She did manage to give me one last glare before whirling on her feet to storm out, dramatically slamming the door behind her.

Once she was gone, my shoulders relaxed. Though it felt wonderful to speak my mind to Mary, I knew that I had destroyed any hope of even a distantly polite relationship between us in the future.

"The future mother-in-law, I assume?" Abe queried.

I straightened, turning to glare at Abe, whom I had almost forgotten was there. I could tell that he was trying to appear mildly concerned, but the corners of his lips twitched as he suppressed an amused smile.

"You shouldn't have come down," I muttered, moving past him towards the stairs. "That woman doesn't need another reason to hate me."

"My sincere apologies, but it did seem like you needed help," Abe said, trying to sound genuine despite the faint note of humor in his tone.

As we headed up the stairs, my irritation at Mary's visit dissipated, and I turned to face him with an apologetic smile.

"I don't care what Mary or anyone thinks. It is

quite late. You can stay the night in one of the guest rooms if you'd like."

Only a few hours ago, I would have been horrified at the thought of having any man stay the night at my home, no matter how innocent, for fear of how the scandal would affect the Harkers. But the night's events now made all those concerns seem trivial, and I was still feeling defiant in the face of Mary's insufferable propriety.

"Now that is the Mina Murray I know," Abe said, returning my smile with a wink. "Thank you. I may end up sleeping in Robert's study—if I sleep at all. It has been some time since I have read through his older research; it is extensive. He–he had a brilliant mind."

Abe looked distant for a moment, his eyes briefly darkening with grief. Abe's own father had died when he was very young. My father had filled that role in his life, and I knew how much Abe had loved him.

On impulse, I reached out to rest my hand on his shoulder in a gesture of comfort. Besides Clara, Abe was the only other person who shared my deep grief over Father's death. It was my combined guilt and grief in the aftermath of Father's death that had caused the dissolution of our relationship, but his death still linked us.

Abe's hand drifted up to rest over mine, and once again heat coursed through me at his touch. Realizing how close we now stood to each other, I took a step back and dropped my hand. There was a brief flicker of some emotion I could not identify in Abe's features before it was gone again, and he turned to head back towards the study.

"Abe, I forgot to mention . . . Father's most recent journal is missing. I haven't been able to find it anywhere. It must have been misplaced. If you were searching for it, you won't find it in there," I said, as the memory of Father's missing journal surfaced.

Abe halted in his tracks, looking back at me with a frown.

"I was looking for it. That is quite odd," he said, puzzled. He stood there for a moment, his brow furrowed, before turning to head back to the study.

Back in my bedroom, Clara had already completed packing my traveling bag, and gave me an approving nod as I entered.

"Good for you, speakin' your mind ta Mary Harker," Clara said, and I realized that she must have heard our entire exchange.

"I'm going to have to apologize," I said grudgingly. "Though she'll never forgive me."

"Tell me wha' happened tonight. Everythin'," Clara said, waving away all talk of Mary Harker. She took my hand and guided me to the bed, taking a seat opposite me.

Clara knew of the tales of vampires that Abe, Father and I had collected during our travels in Transylvania; and she was very aware of how

Father died. But we'd never discussed the possibility of vampires truly existing, and I had maintained that everything that happened in Transylvania had a rational explanation.

Now, I was nervous as I told her everything that happened—from Abe's confronting me on the street to the events at the ball and the aftermath, including Abe's hypnosis of Lucy. Clara remained silent as I spoke. When I finished, she was silent and pale, and not looking at me.

"I know it sounds as if I've gone mad," I said, flustered by her silence. "But I know what I saw, and—"

"I believe you," Clara interrupted. But she still looked uneasy, and her hands were now clenched nervously in her lap.

"Then what is it?" I asked.

Clara remained silent for a long moment, and when her eyes finally met mine, they were wide with agitation.

"Don't go back ta Transylvania, Mina. You can't," she said. "Let the police find him. Please."

"I just told you why we can't rely on the authorities," I said, stunned by her vehemence.

"I knew. I knew this day'd come," she whispered rawly, closing her eyes.

"What do you mean?" I asked. "Clara?"

"Your father," she said heavily, her eyes now filling with tears. "He made me promise ta never tell you this. May God forgive me for breakin' my promise."

"What... what promise?" I asked, my body going cold with dread.

Clara got to her feet and began to pace the room.

"Before your father left for his final trip, he pulled me aside. He looked scared. He told me... he told me no matter wha' happen'd, I was ta never allow you ta return ta Transylvania, nor tell you about his wish," she said. "I gave him my word, but he still wouldn't give me t' reason why," Clara continued. "When you told me he'd died..."

She pressed her hands to her mouth, shutting her eyes as tears began to fall. I wanted to comfort her, but I was frozen with astonishment at her words.

"I wanted ta tell you then, but I remembered t' look on his face. He said no matter wha'. It was like he knew he wouldn't come back, 'n he wanted ta protect you," Clara whispered, looking at me with tearful eyes. "I prayed you'd never have cause ta return to Transylvania."

I recalled how strangely Father had acted before his last trip. He told me he was going to attend a lecture at the Hungarian Academy of Sciences in Budapest. But Father was a terrible liar, and he had barely been able to meet my eyes when he informed me of this. I'd known that he was hiding something. I confided in Abe, and together we decided to follow him to try and determine what he was really up to. When we arrived at the village where he stayed for the night, it was too late.

I had long since concluded that he'd gone to Transylvania to research the veracity of vampires' existence in the region, and he didn't want to tell me or Abe because of our mutual skepticism. But with Clara's words, I now knew there was something more. Father somehow knew that I would want—or need—to return to Transylvania. Why? What had he been hiding? And why hadn't he told me any of this?

As my shock faded, it was replaced by a sense of betrayal and anger. I'd been close with Father, and I always assumed he never hid anything from me. Clara should have told me. If I had known, perhaps I would have begun investigating vampires years ago instead of immersing myself in denial.

I looked up at Clara, my face hot with anger, but her agonized expression quelled my indignation.

Clara was quite loyal. She had always been extremely protective of me, and she just wanted to honor my father and his wishes. It was no fault of her own that he held her to such a promise.

Her desperate eyes were trained on my face, her body stiff, as if bracing herself for my anger. I got to my feet, stepping forward to embrace her. I felt her shoulders sag with relief, and she leaned in to my embrace.

"I'm sorry, Mina. Robert loved you, 'n he seemed so frightened for you."

"It's all right, Clara. I just . . . I just wish he had confided in me," I said, releasing her.

My shock, anger and sense of betrayal had now given way to a heavy fatigue. There was no time to come to terms with all that had happened tonight, and I needed to rest before the next day's journey.

"I need to sleep before we leave," I said, stifling a yawn.

"You're still goin'?" Clara asked, her formerly apologetic tone now sharp with disbelief and a hint of anger. "Mina, your father—"

"Is gone," I bit out, a sharp pain searing my chest at the words. "His secrecy has served no benefit. He is dead, Jonathan's been abducted, and a threat I didn't want to believe exists is here in London. If Father wanted to keep me safe, he should have been honest with me. Transylvania is where the answers are, and where Jonathan's been taken. And that is where I must go."

10

THE DEMETER

I slept fitfully, my dreams filled with images of Jonathan's disoriented face, the vampire's black gaze, and the thick fog surrounding the carriage before it vanished on the bridge.

I awoke just as the first rays of sunlight filtered into my bedroom. I slowly sat up, my eyes still heavy with fatigue. But when the memories of the previous night's events flooded my mind, I stumbled out of bed.

I washed and put on a beige traveling dress, securing my hair in a bun and topping it with a hat before heading to the dining room with my packed bag.

Clara and Abe were already dining on a breakfast of muffins, fruit, cold meat and tea. They both seemed to have slept as little as I had; Abe's eyes were bleary as he gave me a nod of greeting. He excused himself to get us a cab, but before he left

Clara gave him a warm farewell embrace. She murmured something in his ear, and he stiffened at whatever was said, before slipping from the room.

"What did you tell him?" I asked, once he left and we were alone.

"Somethin' he already knows," she said cryptically, placing a warm cup of tea in my hands. Her eyes were shuttered; I knew that she had no intention of divulging what she said to Abe.

"I've left several notes in my room," I said, returning to the matter at hand. "One is for Horace, explaining my absence so he can make arrangements for a substitute to take my place while I'm away. The second is for any general visitors who might call. The third is a very reluctant note of apology to Mary Harker," I added, attempting a bit of levity as I gave her a small smile.

"When'll you be back home?" Clara asked, not at all amused, her face tight with worry.

"When I have Jonathan," I replied. Clara searched my eyes, but the determination she saw in them made her fall silent. She expelled a weary sigh and reached out to touch my cheek, giving me a sad smile.

"You've always been stubborn . . . even when you were just a lass," she said. "Please be safe."

"I will," I replied solemnly, reaching up to squeeze her hand.

Moments later, Clara stood in the doorway, watching as I climbed into a cab next to Abe. Her face was pale with anxiety, and she didn't return the reassuring smile I gave her as the cab clattered away.

When our cab dropped us at the entrance to the port of Tilbury in Essex, Seward was already there, his bag at his side. His hands were shoved deep into his pockets, his features marred with fretfulness. After exchanging polite greetings, we waited for Arthur.

It seemed as if we were waiting for quite some time, and I was starting to wonder if Arthur had decided against coming when the Holmwood carriage approached, pulling to a stop directly in front of us. The carriage driver stepped out to open the passenger door.

Arthur exited, his arm around Lucy, who moved stiffly in tandem with her husband. Her eyes were back to their natural brown, though they were dazed and fatigued. She was smartly dressed in a forest green traveling dress, her brown hair secured in a bun, and the veiled hat that rested on her head partially obstructed her face. The only thing off about her appearance was her oddly pale skin and the jerky movement of her limbs; Arthur seemed to completely shoulder her weight as they moved.

"I gave her the sedative you prescribed," Arthur said to Abe as they reached us. "Once we are on the ship, I will have to give her an additional dosage. I fear it is the only way to keep her calm."

"I understand," Abe said, looking at Lucy with

concern.

"Our journey is only a few hours," Arthur continued, now addressing us all. "But in his message to me this morning, Captain Harper informed me that we can make use of his and two officers' cabins for the duration. That will allow us a place to discuss our—present dilemma—without being overheard . . . and I can keep Lucy away from curious eyes."

I studied Lucy, whose head was now resting on Abe's shoulder, her visage bearing the eerie calm of the heavily sedated. There was no trace of the dangerous creature who had lunged at me the previous night. Her cool brown eyes slid to me, and I thought I saw something dark shift in her eyes, like a dragon being stirred from its slumber, before it was gone again, and I swiftly looked away.

We headed through the port, which was bustling at this early hour. Ships of various sizes clogged the harbor, their pointed masts clustered so closely together that I was reminded of a forest of pine trees. Dockhands and cranes alike loaded crates of cargo on to the anchored ships, while even more ships drifted into the harbor. The air here was damp with the salty muskiness of the Thames, the sky gray with the promise of a storm.

As we walked, I once again felt a cold prickle on the back of my neck. It was the same sensation I'd felt at both the cemetery and the ball, and I stopped in my tracks, whirling to scan the port.

"Mina? Are you all right?" Abe asked. He and the others had halted as well, regarding me with concerned frowns.

I took another look around, but other than curious glances from some of the dockhands, there appeared to be nothing or no one out of the ordinary. The sensation was gone now, and I wondered if the feeling had just been in my mind. Perhaps my fatigue and anxiety from all that had transpired the night before made me abnormally aware of my surroundings.

"Yes," I said hastily, hurrying forward to join them, but Abe's perceptive gaze lingered on my face.

We approached the *Demeter*, the largest of the ships anchored, looming above the rest like a mighty colossus, its sails fluttering in the light breeze. A harried young man approached, removing his hat at the sight of me and Lucy. He looked like a boy stretched to a man's height, with a spattering of freckles, a mop of ginger hair, and green eyes that shone with both youth and kindness.

"Mister Holmwood?" he asked. At Arthur's nod, he continued. "I'm George, first mate. The captain said I'm ta take care of ya. I'll escort ya t'your quarters. Afraid they're a bit rough," he added apologetically. "But 'tis only for a few hours. We rarely take passengers across the Channel."

"That is quite all right," Arthur politely

returned. "We are grateful to be accommodated on such short notice."

George took my bag and led us across the gangway, across the wide deck of the ship and down the steep ladders that led to the cabins.

Arthur and Lucy were to share the captain's cabin, while Abe and Seward settled into George's cabin, and I stayed in the second officers' cabin. My cabin was not as run down as we had been warned, and though it was minuscule, I found it rather quaint, furnished with a small bed and desk, and smelling of the sweat of the sea.

I set my bag down onto the narrow bed, reaching inside to unearth a betrothal photograph of myself and Jonathan that I'd carefully packed. In the photograph, Jonathan and I sat next to each other, gazing politely at the camera.

I remembered the day we took the photograph well. I had hated the whole affair, with Mary hovering behind the photographer, constantly ordering me to adjust my posture and sit like a proper lady. Jonathan kept me at ease the entire time by whispering jokes into my ear; I could now detect a faint trace of a smile that tugged at my lips in the photo.

Taking in Jonathan's image, I traced the outline of his face, filled with a sudden surge of worry and dread. Where was he right now?

I will bring you home safe, Jonathan, I thought. *I promise.*

When I went up to the main deck, I found Arthur standing alone by the rails, his expression distant as he watched the activity of the port below. I hesitated, not wanting to disturb him, and I started to turn back around.

"Mina. Please," he said, gesturing to the empty spot next to him. "Your presence would be agreeable."

I obliged him, and we stood in companionable silence for a moment, taking in the Thames and the bustle of the port around us, before he spoke.

"My father did not want me to marry Lucy," he said. I was startled by such a personal revelation, considering that we had only just been acquainted, but I remained silent. "He thought her family was not suitable enough to be paired with the Holmwoods. I did not care. She was full of life. It was as if the sun itself followed her wherever she went..." he trailed off, and then blinked, as if surprised that he had spoken his thoughts out loud. "My apologies, Mina. I do not usually speak so plainly. Please do not feel as if you have to—"

"There's no need to apologize," I interrupted gently, giving him a kind smile. "Please. Tell me about her."

"Lucy wanted children quite desperately," he continued, after a long pause. "That is what our row was about. We had only just been married. I wanted to wait until my business had grown a bit. Lucy was always passionate, and she often stormed out during our rows. When she left this last time, I did not think to go after her right away; I was quite angry myself. When she did not return . . ." he trailed off again, his pale eyes glistening with tears. "If I had just gone after her."

"You didn't know, Arthur," I said. "You couldn't have possibly known."

Arthur didn't respond, taking off his spectacles to clean them with a handkerchief before returning his focus to the port.

"We went on holiday to Venice last year. We were walking along the Grand Canal to watch the sunset, and she turned to me, her eyes were filled with tears. I asked her what was the matter. She told me that she had never been more happy; that she wanted to remember that moment forever. I keep wondering . . . did she know? Did she know what would happen to her?"

"You'll have your happy moments again," I insisted, my heart aching for him.

"You do not have to say that," Arthur replied, with a sad smile. "We do not even understand what this is. I know her chances of recovery are minute. There have been moments of lucidity, when she is still my Lucy. This morning, as I got her dressed, she looked at me, and she said, 'Arthur, you have to let me go. I cannot live like this.'" His voice broke. "But you were right, Mina. She would have wanted to help. She had—has—a kind soul. We take much for granted," he continued, with a sigh. "We assume that everything we have will always remain so. There is still hope for you and your Jonathan. God willing, my Lucy can help you find him."

"Thank you," I whispered, both moved by his words and praying that he was right; that there was hope for Jonathan.

We fell into a solemn silence. Seward and Abe soon came up onto the deck to join us, and the captain approached us. Captain William Harper was a grizzled man in his fifties, with graying black hair and a thick untamed beard. He had the rough weathered look of a man who spent more of his life at sea than on land, but his gray eyes were amiable, and I took an instant liking to him.

"Thank you for providing us transport to Calais," Arthur said politely, giving him a grateful smile.

"I am happy to help. Your father was a friend," Captain Harper replied. "You and your friends are my honored guests. I must warn you, these skies have me nervous. There was no sign of a storm when we arrived this morning. I'm certain we can get across the Channel before it hits. We should arrive in Calais later this afternoon. I hope you get to your relative in time," he added, his voice softening with sympathy.

Arthur had informed Captain Harper that we needed to get to France as quickly as possible to visit a sick relative. It was a necessary lie, as we could hardly tell him the real reason for our need to leave England so hastily.

"We hope so as well, thank you," Arthur said, holding Captain Harper's eyes, giving away no indication of the lie.

"George will come and fetch you from your cabins for a late breakfast," Captain Harper said. "I should warn you, I have a large crew for this journey, and many of them have taken ill with fever; they're mostly confined to the sailors' berths. You are all free to move about the ship at will, just avoid the berths, the illness is contagious."

After he left us, we went down to his cabin to talk without the risk of being overheard. The cabin was the largest of the three we'd settled in, yet it could still barely fit all three of us. Lucy was sleeping when we entered, her body curled protectively beneath the thin blanket, facing away from us. Arthur sat down on the bed next to her, careful not to disturb her sleeping form. Seward and I remained next to the door, while Abe moved over to the small desk and perched on its edge.

"There is still much we do not know," Abe said. "When I experiment, I begin with what I do know."

"We do the same with our investigations," Seward said. "Start with the facts and work backwards."

"Well, we know that Jonathan was abducted

from the Langham last night by vampires. Who else was taken?" I asked.

"Nicholas Lewiston, Edward Johnson, and Fannie Herman," Seward replied, reciting from memory. "I went to Scotland Yard before I came home last night to see if there was any new information. Mister Lewiston and Johnson are solicitors; Fannie Herman was a maid in the cloakroom. Their families are devastated. They don't know why anyone would abduct them, and they doubted they'd just leave London without telling anyone."

I frowned, baffled. What would vampires want with a cloakroom maid and three solicitors?

"Jonathan's law partner wanted to discuss something with him, right before he was abducted," I said, recalling how Peter Hawkins had pulled him aside. "And he mentioned that there were robberies at his office."

"Can you send a wire to Mister Hawkins when we get to Calais—find out what they discussed?" Seward asked. "If any of it's related, it could help us determine why he was taken."

I nodded, and Abe continued, speaking quickly now, as if his words were scrambling to keep pace with his thoughts. "The Ripper murders go back several years, and they are still occurring, unbeknownst to the public. The victims are the poor and wealthy alike. Right around the time the Ripper murders began, there were accounts of other murders and disappearances all throughout

Europe. Berlin, Paris, Amsterdam . . . a fortnight ago, Lucy was bitten by a vampire. Now, there could be many explanations. The murders could just be that—murders. I know from lore, my research, and witness accounts that vampires need blood to survive. Naturally, they would kill their victims to obtain their blood—and there is reproduction, of course. All biological forms reproduce, that could explain why they have moved from the countryside to the cities. More humans to transform."

"Why the abductions?" I asked. "It's not necessary to abduct someone for the transformation to take hold—look at Lucy."

Another silence fell, and I closed my eyes to concentrate. I recalled a technique Father had once taught me when I struggled to solve a difficult mathematical equation one of my tutors had me solve. *Use the heuristic method*, Father had told me. *Think of the simplest solution. With every problem, it is always the simplest solution.*

Abductions, murders, reproduction, the pack mentality of vampires, the—

My eyes flew open as the answer to my question came to me. How could I have not seen this before? It was the simplest answer to our questions, but the most horrifying one.

I recalled Lucy's words from the night before. *We need them.*

"*Godsamme*," Abe whispered, a Dutch oath he

rarely uttered. His stunned gaze met mine. He had come to the same conclusion.

"What?" Seward asked, looking back and forth between me and Abe with alarm.

"They've moved from the countrysides to cities," I said, my voice trembling with dread. "Because they're increasing their numbers."

"Yes, we've gathered that," Seward said shortly. "What is the—"

"What reason would they have to multiply so expeditiously?" Abe asked. "Only four years ago, Robert, Mina and I learned of the murders in the Transylvanian countryside. But there were very few—if any—mentions of actual disappearances. During the past three years, the unexplained disappearances have dramatically increased. Think. What possible reason could they have to abduct so many? We know from Lucy that the transformation takes time. It is obvious that they want to increase their numbers. Why so quickly? To what end?"

Arthur and Seward's eyes locked with ours as they were hit with the same realization. Arthur blanched, and Seward leaned back heavily against the wall, burying his face in his hands.

"Bloody hell," Seward whispered. This time, he was too shocked to apologize to me for the oath. "No."

"They're building an army," I said, finally speaking aloud the terrible words that we were all thinking.

11

INVASION

On the deck above, the ship's crew shouted directions to each other as it began to pull away from the docks to drift down the churning waters of the Thames towards the Channel. But the captain's cabin was filled with a roaring silence.

"The only reason to have an army is to invade—and we can't stop a bloody invasion on our own," Seward said, splintering the silence. "If this theory's right, then everything's changed."

"I agree," I said. "But it hasn't happened yet, which means we have time to stop it."

"Did you not hear me?" Seward demanded, his voice rising with incredulity. "How can we possibly—"

"Every army has a leader. If you destroy the leader—" I began.

"You destroy the army," Abe concluded. "If there is a leader, we can attempt to confirm his identity through Lucy. Our goal is still the same, Jack," he said to Seward. "We rescue Jonathan and whoever else they've taken—and kill the creature who abducted them. If the abductor and this leader are one and the same, killing him can possibly scatter his followers and prevent an invasion before it happens. By then, perhaps we will have gathered enough proof of vampires to involve the authorities."

"If we fail—" Seward began.

"We can't," I interrupted, shivering at the thought.

"But if we do," Seward repeated, scowling at me. "I want a safeguard. No, my colleagues won't believe me now if I tell them an invasion of vampires is likely upon us. But I want to at least send them a wire warning them of an imminent threat to London. I'll think of a way to word it. That way they can be vigilant and prepared."

Abe and I nodded our agreement. Seward visibly relaxed, though he still looked disturbed.

"Arthur," Abe said. Arthur had been so silent that I'd almost forgotten he was there. He looked dazed with trepidation at our exchange, and shakily met Abe's eyes. "I need to wake Lucy to communicate through her."

Arthur seemed to emerge from his daze,

turning towards Lucy to wake her, but she began to stir on her own. We all stilled as she sat up, turning to face us.

I had to stifle a gasp at the sight of her. The whites of her eyes had again gone black, and she seemed to look right through us.

"Arthur, step back," Abe said, speaking slowly and calmly, though his voice wavered. Arthur was staring at his wife in frozen shock, but he obliged Abe, stumbling aback from the bed as Abe stepped tentatively forward, pulling the silver locket from his coat pocket. I noticed that one hand had strayed behind his back, clutching the hilt of a knife that was nestled in his back pocket.

"Lucy," Abe said. "Are you there?"

"She's gone," Lucy expelled on a sigh, her voice light as a feather. "It's only me now. Me and my brethren. Your Lucy will never return to you."

Her brethren? Dread stirred within me at her words. Arthur sucked in his breath, his face going white, while Seward stiffened, clenching his hands into fists at his sides.

Abe was the only one of us who appeared calm. Keeping his eyes trained on her, he lifted up the locket to her eye level; but she paid it no mind, her black eyes intent on his face.

"You have a leader," Abe pressed. "Who is he?"

Lucy smiled, the sight a horrible thing, revealing her unnaturally sharp teeth.

"The last of the Old Families . . . two as one," Lucy whispered. "All will be made new again," she added cryptically, a delirious smile spreading across her face.

I shuddered at her ominous words. I still wanted to ask her about Jonathan—why he'd been taken and if he was unharmed, but the threat of violence in her eyes held me back, and I was fearful for Abe. He was within striking distance of her, and she was unrestrained.

"I know what you desire," she continued, her voice dangerous as she looked at Abe. "But we will not be stopped."

"What are—" Abe began, but he abruptly went stiff, his arms limply falling to his sides, the locket clattering to the floor.

I realized with horror that she had somehow taken control of him, and had put him under some sort of paralysis. I recalled the paralysis Abe and I had been put under the night of Father's death. The same thing was being done to Abe now; I was certain of it.

"Lucy!" Arthur cried, stumbling forward. "Lucy, stop it! Come back to me! Lucy!"

But Lucy's eyes never left Abe's, and I saw her eyes slide hungrily to his throat.

No, I thought in a panic, instinctively lunging forward. I was unarmed, my kukri knives were stowed in my cabin, so I moved towards the knife in

Abe's back pocket. But Arthur lurched forward to grab my arm, holding me back.

"Let me go—" I cried, struggling in his grasp.

"You will not harm her!" Arthur shouted.

"Arthur, that's not your bloody wife!" Seward shouted, darting forward to reach for Abe's knife.

Our commotion had caught Lucy's attention, and her scrutiny shifted away from Abe and towards us.

As soon as her eyes left him, Abe was released from his paralysis, and before Seward or I could reach him, he moved quickly, lunging forward to inject a syringe he had hidden in his hand into the soft flesh of her neck. She let out a vicious snarl as Seward scrambled forward to hold her down, and Abe injected her with yet another dosage of the sedative. She finally went still, her eyes glazing over before fluttering shut, her breathing painful and ragged as she fell into a deep sleep.

Arthur sank to his knees, closing his eyes as Abe and Seward secured her wrists to the bedposts with handcuffs that Seward had brought with him. When they stepped back, Arthur spoke, still eyeing her with unease.

"Abraham," he whispered. "Is my wife gone?"

Abe stepped forward, placing a hand on his friend's shoulder.

"Yes," he replied. "I believe we just witnessed

the last stage of her transformation. She is no longer your Lucy."

Arthur pressed his hand to his mouth and began to weep. It was a heartbreaking sight, and once again my heart ached for him as he raised tearful eyes to Abe. Yet I couldn't disagree with Abe's conclusion. There had been no traces of humanity in Lucy's black eyes.

"I had hope," Arthur said, when his tears subsided and he climbed back to his feet. "That we could cure her somehow."

"Do not blame yourself, Arthur," Abe said, his eyes heavy with regret. "I should never have insisted that you bring her."

"Nor should I," I said, feeling a pang of guilt as I recalled how I had convinced him to bring Lucy. "I'm so sorry, Arthur."

"Once we arrive in Calais, please allow me to pay for your passage back to London." Abe said.

"That will not be necessary. I–I do not believe she will make it that far. I cannot keep her restrained in the company of others. We will attract too much attention."

"We can find you an inn in Calais," Abe said, after a brief pause. "Take the time you feel is necessary."

He met Arthur's eyes, his dark meaning clear. Arthur was going to kill the creature that his wife had become.

"If you need help, I can—" Abe continued with great difficulty, but Arthur held up his hand.

"No," Arthur said. "It has to be me. I am her husband. It . . . it will break my heart, but it is what she would have wanted."

My eyes slid towards Lucy's sleeping form. In her slumber, I could see traces of the beautiful human woman she'd once been, and I was pierced with a pang of sorrow for her and Arthur. But trepidation lurked beneath my empathy. *What if Jonathan's been turned?* I wondered. I had to get to him before that could happen.

There was a knock at the door, and Abe had the wherewithal to quickly cover Lucy's handcuffs with blankets and a pillow before Seward swung open the door.

George stood there, looking surprised to find us all in the cabin.

"There's food in the wardroom," he said, his tone polite despite his obvious puzzlement. "Captain wanted me ta inform ya the storm's almost upon us . . . couldn't avoid it. The wind's pushing us off course towards the North Sea. We'll be delayed in getting ta Calais. Rest of the journey'll be a bit choppy."

I turned to glance out the small cabin window. I had been so distracted by our discussion and then Lucy's near attack that I'd not noticed the now darkened sky and gray choppy waters of the sea.

My heart plummeted. The longer our delay, the longer it would take to get to Jonathan.

George left, and we started to file out after him, but Arthur remained behind.

"You should not stay in here alone," Abe said, looking anxiously at Lucy's unconscious form. "Let Seward or I—"

"I want to spend what little time I have left with her, even if she is lost to me," Arthur replied, his eyes filled with anguish. "I have the morphia sedative and . . . and one of your knives just in case."

We reluctantly left him behind, making our way across the corridor to the wardroom. We had it to ourselves, and a small meal of coffee, biscuits, and marmalade had been set up for us at the long table, somehow managing to stay in place despite the rocking of the ship.

As we ate, my mind kept returning to Lucy's transformation and her ominous words.

"What do you think Lucy meant?" I asked. "Last of the Old Families? Her brethren?"

"I think she confirmed your theory," Seward replied. "Those vamp—" he stopped himself, closing his eyes. "I can't even say the bloody word. Sorry," he added quickly to me, as soon as he uttered the oath. "*Vampires* are planning to take over, and they have a leader."

"If we could just confirm the name of their

leader," I said. "When we're on land, perhaps we can get more information from Lu—"

"We cannot risk communicating with her anymore," Abe interjected. "The sedative barely worked on her and it is the strongest one I have access to. I cannot control her through hypnosis anymore."

I reluctantly fell silent; he was right. I had come very close to using Abe's knife against her. But I felt a rush of helplessness. Lucy had been my only way of keeping track of Jonathan. I could only pray that she had set us in the right direction.

"What we need to know is how to kill them," Seward said. "Besides silver, what're their weaknesses?"

"The villagers in Transylvania mentioned crosses, garlic—" I began.

"No. They may have been right about vampires, but not about the means of destroying them. Those are mere superstitions," Abe said. "Lucy had no reaction when I held up a cross. It was the same with garlic. She took it from me and ate it. Stabbing vampires in the heart can kill them instantly. Beheading works as well. There may be—"

Abe abruptly fell silent as Captain Harper entered the wardroom, his crinkled face marred with concern.

"It's going to get rougher with these winds. You'll likely be more comfortable in the cabins. In my experience, sudden storms like these usually die down quickly. Once it does, I can get us back on course."

We nodded and thanked him, but I was far more worried about the delay than the choppiness of our journey.

We obliged the captain, resolving to ride out the storm in our cabins and to get as much rest as we could before hitting land.

Once I was alone in my cabin, I reached into my bag to remove one of Father's journals. Since I had been unable to locate his most recent journal, I had taken several other of his journals with me, hoping to stumble upon something of importance.

The entry I skimmed through was an account of a biology conference he attended in Brussels several months prior to his death, but there was nothing of note in the entry.

I closed the journal, frowning. I found it odd that none of his entries mentioned his research into vampires or his trips to Transylvania—I knew he had taken several in the year prior to his death. The entries were brief and perfunctory, but Father had been a detailed observer and note-taker.

Had he purposefully been hiding something? Prior to Clara's revelation, I would have dismissed the thought, but now I wasn't so certain. If so, what had he been hiding? And why?

Fatigue settled over me, quelling my tumultuous thoughts. I wanted to keep reading, and tried to resist the pull of sleep, but I was unable to fight the weight of my exhaustion.

I stretched out on the small bed, resting my head on the small pillow. As I drifted off, Lucy's haunting words flitted through my mind once more. *We will not be stopped.*

WHEN I CAME TO, my cabin was swaying abruptly from side to side by the force of the storm and the sea. There was no window in my room, and I did not know the time.

I groggily sat up, stiffening when I heard a strange sound. Beneath the sound of pattering rain on the ship's hull, I could hear a low rumble outside my door. I sat perfectly still and listened as the rumbling continued.

The sound was not rumbling . . . it was a growl. A growl that sounded eerily similar to the sound Lucy made when she tried to attack me back in London.

Could it be Lucy? Had she gotten free?

On edge, I looked at the door. It was locked, but I knew it wouldn't be able to withstand much force. Panic coiled around me as I closed my eyes, struggling to recall Sofia's words. *Always use fear to your benefit, Mina. Never allow it to hinder you.*

I forced myself to my feet, and crept over to my bag, taking out my two kukri knives. I stowed one in my sleeve and kept the other in my hand. Steadying my breathing, I moved silently to the door, and placed my hand on the latch.

I listened. I could still hear faint growling. It seemed to come from further down the corridor.

I silently counted to three before I swung open the door, ready to fight.

12

OVERRUN

I froze at the sight that met my eyes at the end of the corridor.

A shipmate crouched in an animalistic position over the still, prone body of George, feasting on his blood. His teeth were sunk into George's throat, his eyes closed with bliss as he drank, droplets of blood spilling from the sides of his mouth. It was an uncanny recreation of what I'd seen the night of Father's murder.

A hand clamped over my mouth and strong arms wrapped around me from behind, dragging me back into my cabin. Fear coursed through me, and once the arms released me, I whirled around, raising my kukri to strike.

I lowered my kukri as I realized it was only Abe, looking as shaken as I felt. He carried his, Seward's and Arthur's bags, the straps wrapped around his shoulders, a large knife tucked into his front pocket. He placed a finger to his lips, and gently but firmly pushed me aside to close the door, pressing his body against it.

"The captain mentioned his shipmates being ill," Abe whispered, his face white. "*That* is the illness."

"Oh, no," I whispered. I did recall Captain Harper mentioning ill shipmates, but I never would have thought...

"How—" I began.

"We will have to ponder that later. Right now, we need to get off this ship. There are dozens of shipmates aboard, and there is no telling how many have been transformed. Seward was not in the cabin when I awoke from my nap. Arthur and Lucy's cabin is empty as well. Gather what you can. We must leave."

Reeling with shock, I moved to grab my bag, and kept my rising panic at bay. Abe handed me two knives from his bag, which I tucked securely into my bodice and my other sleeve before slinging my bag securely over my shoulder. I gave Abe a quick nod to indicate that I was ready, my kukri in hand.

"Walk quickly. Do not run. It is my hope that we can get to the upper deck without the vampire noticing," Abe said.

My heart pounded wildly as Abe opened the door and we stepped out of my cabin, not daring to look behind us as we moved down the narrow corridor. The ship rocked with the force of the sea, and it took great effort not to stumble as I walked, especially given my terror. Behind us, I could hear the sickening slurping sounds as the creature continued to feast on George, and I had to suppress my nausea and revulsion at the sound.

As we neared the stairs at the end of the corridor, a warning snarl behind us indicated that we'd been seen. I knew that we could not outrun him, and Abe seemed to share my thoughts.

We both halted, and turned around.

The vampire had lifted his head up from George's neck, his mouth stained with blood, his black pupils trained on us. From his smooth skin and lanky frame, I surmised that he must have once been a boyish young man like George, full of life. Any trace of humanity had long gone. He bared his teeth, revealing front incisors that were elongated into sharp fangs. He slowly rose to his full height, like a cobra poising for a fatal strike.

Paralyzing fear held me rigid as his black eyes met ours, darkly similar to Lucy's. Abe moved into a defensive stance, stepping in front of me as he took out his knife.

"Mina, run," he whispered, his focus trained on the vampire.

"I'm not leaving you," I protested, stepping out from behind him and moving into a defensive stance of my own as I clutched my kukri.

There was no time to for him to protest.

Instead, we kept our eyes on the vampire as he began to stalk towards us, his movements oddly controlled and civilized for a creature who had just feasted on blood. His eyes swept from Abe towards me, and I detected an eagerness in the soulless depths of his eyes; a look of unbridled anticipation and bloodlust. I had to force myself to remain stock still as he drew near.

As he came within striking distance, Abe and I lifted our weapons, but before we could strike, a knife sailed past us and lodged itself directly in the vampire's heart.

The vampire stiffened, his black eyes shifting back to a very human shade of brown, looking down at the knife now embedded in his chest before he sank to his knees and slumped to the floor.

Stunned, we whirled around. A man stood on the ladder behind us, his eyes locked on the vampire's now still form. He was tall and broad shouldered, with light cinnamon skin that indicated both Turkish and European ancestry. With his black hair and silver eyes, he had the look of an avenging angel.

"You need to get off this ship," he said curtly, his English perfect and bearing no trace of an accent. He barely looked at us as he descended the remaining steps. He moved past us to bend down over the dead vampire, yanking the knife out of his chest. "It has been overrun with newborn vampires.

There's a jolly boat on the upper deck. Take it to get off the ship."

Thunderstruck, Abe and I just stared at him. He referred to vampires as casually as one would refer to the weather. Who was he? And how did he know about vampires?

I studied him closely. There was something familiar about him, though I didn't recognize him from the shipmates we'd seen so far, and I had no doubt I would have remembered him.

"Leave," he repeated, straightening to glare at us. "Do you want to get yourselves killed?"

Without waiting for our response, he moved past us to head back up the stairs. We exchanged a bewildered glance, emerging from our shock to dash after him.

"Who are you?" I stammered, as we made our way up the ladder towards the upper deck.

"There's no time for introductions. You need to get off this ship," he replied. "Your friends are up on deck as well—take them with you. I'll distract the monsters."

He left no time for further questions, hurrying up the remainder of the steps to the deck and leaving us behind.

We scrambled after him, a multitude of questions racing through my mind about his identity, but I pushed them aside. It was best to heed his words and get off this ship. I could find out who he was later.

When we reached the upper deck, we halted. It was as if we had stumbled into a waking nightmare.

The raging storm had turned the late-afternoon sky dark and ominous, and sheets of rain now poured down onto the chaotic scene. Dozens of transformed shipmates swarmed the deck, their eyes black and fangs elongated as they attacked and feasted on the surviving human shipmates. I watched in dazed fright as two newborn vampires crouched over a dying and bleeding shipmate, eagerly feasting from his throat. Another vampire leapt onto a shipmate as he tried to flee, tearing into his chest with his fangs. On the opposite side of the deck, several terrified shipmates leapt overboard before they could be attacked by a pursuing vampire.

Amidst the chaos, I could see Seward on the far side of the deck by the railing, protectively standing in front of a terrified Captain Harper and several shipmates, warding off any approaching vampires by firing his revolver into their hearts. All around him, other shipmates tried in vain to fight off the attacking vampires with knives, their cries of terror rising above the furious staccato pounding of raindrops on the deck.

As Abe and I stood there rooted to the spot in horror, two vampires charged towards us from the center of the deck. At the sight of them, we were pulled from our shock, and once again Abe moved to stand protectively in front of me.

The mysterious man who had rescued us on the lower deck darted out from behind us, moving in front of their eye line and directing their attention towards him. He turned and raced towards the ship's mast, leading them away from us.

We raced towards Seward, slashing our weapons at any vampires who lunged towards us as we ran. We quickly reached Seward's side, moving into defensive stances to continue warding off any approaching vampires.

"We need to leave!" I shouted, slashing wildly at the throat of a vampire as he lunged towards me. "Where's Arthur? Lucy?!"

"I don't know! And I don't know how much longer we can hold these bloody things off!" Seward shouted, firing his revolver at another charging vampire.

I looked around and spotted Lucy and Arthur standing by the main hatch. Even through the heavy rain, I could see that Lucy was fully vampire now, her pale skin pulled even more tautly over her bones, her black eyes intense as she focused on Arthur. He stood opposite her, looking as entranced as Jonathan had before he was abducted at the Langham.

"Jack, take Mina and the others to the jolly boat!" Abe shouted, following my gaze towards Arthur and Lucy. "I am going to get Arthur!"

"Abe, no!" I cried, but he had already left our defensive perimeter, and raced through the swarm of clashing human and vampire bodies towards Arthur and Lucy.

Ignoring Seward's shout of warning, I charged after him. A vampire launched himself at me as I ran, knocking me down and pinning me to the deck. He reared down towards my throat, his teeth bared, but I managed to evade him, turning my head away as I acted on pure instinct and lodged my kukri into the side his neck. Dark crimson spurted from the wound, and he stiffened as I yanked the blade out of his neck before sinking it directly into his heart.

I had never killed before, and the dark pleasure I felt at the act shocked me as the vampire went still and lifeless.

I shoved him off of me, stumbling back to my feet and dashing towards Abe, who now stood feet away from Arthur.

"Arthur!" Abe shouted, as I reached his side. "She is not your Lucy! We must go!"

I looked around the deck. Seward was holding off the remaining vampires with his revolver, but they were now focused on the other surviving humans. It was only a matter of time before they turned their attention on us.

"Arthur!" I shouted. "Please! We don't have much time!"

Arthur stood transfixed, his eyes focused on the creature who had once been his wife.

"Arthur, my husband. Help me."

Though Lucy spoke softly, her words somehow carried over the din of the storm and the chaos that surrounded us. Her eyes had turned brown once more, and she was looking at him with seemingly genuine helplessness. "I don't know what is happening to me. Please, my husband. Come. Help me."

Somehow I knew that this was a trick. Lucy was gone; the monster had taken over.

"Arthur, no!" Abe and I cried in unison, as Arthur stepped closer towards her.

Abe started forward to stop him, but Lucy turned towards us, and we were instantly put under paralysis. Forced into stillness, we could only watch helplessly as Arthur continued towards her.

Once he reached her, she wound her long pale fingers in his tawny hair, pulling him towards her. I couldn't bear to watch his inevitable death at her hands, but the paralysis prevented me from closing my eyes, and I was forced to watch as their lips met in a deeply sensual kiss.

As they kissed, I saw Arthur's hand subtly drift to his back pocket, and he pulled out a large knife that rested there; I recognized it as one of Abe's.

It happened quickly. He yanked the knife upwards before sinking it into her heart. Her eyes widened, and for a brief moment she looked human again. I saw a flicker of love and gratitude in her eyes before they fluttered shut, and she slumped to the deck, still in Arthur's arms.

Abe and I were instantly released from our paralysis. We stumbled forward as Arthur held her close, his eyes wet with tears.

"Forgive me, my angel," Arthur whispered rawly, rocking her in his arms. "My Lucy. May God forgive me."

"We have to leave! Now!" Seward cried.

Abe and I turned. The rain had tapered off to a drizzle, and Seward limped towards us. He was supporting a weakened Captain Harper, who bled from an open wound on the side of his throat. The other shipmates Seward had guarded lay dead behind them, and the deck was now still and silent, littered with the dead bodies of both humans and vampires. There was no sign of the mysterious man who had helped us.

"I won't make it," Captain Harper gasped, stumbling to his knees as they reached us. "Take this. It's my observations of odd events on the ship. It may help you."

"We're not leaving you," Seward said, taking the journal as he reached out to steady him.

Captain Harper waved away his help, remaining on his knees, and taking in uneven breaths of air.

"I'll not leave my ship," he said, meeting our eyes. "There may be more of those monsters aboard. You should leave. Quickly."

We hesitated, but the captain's look broached

no argument. Arthur got to his feet, still holding Lucy in his arms.

"Arthur—" Abe protested.

"I will not leave my wife's body behind. I want to bury her myself," Arthur whispered brokenly. Without waiting for a reply, he moved away from us, towards the jolly boat on the opposite side of the deck.

I took one last look at Captain Harper as we trailed behind Arthur. He had moved into a sitting position, his eyes drooping, his breathing short and uneven. His gaze trailed over the bodies strewn across the deck before focusing on the surrounding sea, where it remained until his eyes shut for the final time, and he went completely still before slumping over onto his side.

There was no time to mourn for the kind captain we had known so briefly. As soon as we reached the jolly boat, which hung on the side of the ship by davits, we heard savage snarls behind us.

We whirled. Several vampires had emerged from the far side of the lower deck, standing by the companionway, their hungry eyes centered on us.

"I can hold them off," Arthur said, stepping forward to deposit Lucy's body into a stunned Seward's arms. "Leave."

"Arthur, wait—" Abe protested.

"Leave!" Arthur repeated, already moving away from us, using his knife to cut a jagged wound into his wrist. At the sight of the fresh blood that spilled from the wound, the vampires immediately set their sights on him.

Ignoring our cries of protest, Arthur raced towards the rear of the ship, and the vampires gave chase.

"The fool!" Abe cried, his voice trembling with despair.

"He's made up his mind," I said, grabbing Abe's arm. "We have to go!"

After a brief moment of hesitation, Abe turned and pushed me into the boat, while Seward placed Lucy's body in the center. They both began to lower it into the sea by the attached ropes, their muscles straining with effort. Once it hit the sea, they climbed down the ropes and clamored into the boat, carefully unhooking it from the *Demeter*.

"Wait," Abe said anxiously, once we were all settled into the boat and Seward reached for the oars.

He was looking up at the ship for any sign of Arthur. We waited for several fraught moments, until both Arthur and the man who had rescued us appeared at the ship's edge.

My relief was short-lived when I saw Arthur's physical state. While the mysterious man appeared to be unharmed, though his shirt and skin was splattered with blood, Arthur looked frighteningly pale, bleeding heavily from bite wounds on his neck and shoulders, as well as the cut on his arm.

"Throw him down!" Abe cried, and with surprising strength, the man shouldered Arthur's weight, pushing him over the side. Abe barely managed to catch Arthur, crumbling beneath his weight before lowering him gently to his back in the center of the boat next to Lucy. The man remained where he was on the ship's edge, looking hesitant to join us.

"Come with us!" I shouted. "Quickly!"

But the words had barely left my lips when a vampire appeared behind him, yanking him back on to the ship with ferocious strength.

A second vampire perched himself on the edge of the ship, his hungry black eyes trained on Arthur and his bleeding wounds. Seward began to row away from the ship, but the vampire still eyed us, and I realized his intent with growing apprehension.

The vampire angled his body, preparing to leap off the ship and onto our boat. Seward was rowing quickly, but I knew we wouldn't get away in time—the vampire was only seconds away from leaping onto our boat.

I reached out to yank Abe's knife from his pocket and scrambled to my feet, struggling to maintain my balance in the rocking boat. I carefully angled the knife, and as the vampire leapt, I hurled it in his direction with all my might.

The knife sailed through the air to lodge into

his throat, and the vampire stiffened before dropping into the sea with a splatter.

I remained standing, reaching for the kukri tucked into my sleeve should the vampire resurface, but I could vaguely see the still form of the creature through the murky waters as he sank to the bottom of the sea. The tension in my body dissipated, and I closed my eyes.

Once my breathing returned to normal, I sat back down. Seward gave me a grateful and impressed nod as he continued to row, while Abe desperately tried to stop Arthur's bleeding.

Arthur was deathly pale now, his breathing ragged. Abe looked up to meet my eyes, and I could tell by his troubled features that it was too late. Arthur would not survive.

"We'll soon be at shore," Seward said, as if reading our minds. "We'll get you help, Arthur."

"Abraham. Mina," Arthur rasped, focusing his pained eyes on us.

We leaned in close. Though he was clearly in great agony, a calm had settled over his face, and he reached a hand out towards Lucy's still body, weakly entwining his fingers through hers.

"We're almost at shore," I said, trying to keep my voice steady as I gave him a forced smile. "We're going to get you—"

"Listen to me," Arthur interrupted, holding our gazes. "You find Jonathan. Do not let him suffer the same fate as my Lucy. You— you must find this creature. This monster," he coughed, and even through his weakness and pain, I could sense his rage. "And you destroy him."

"We will destroy him together," Abe said, but his voice quivered, his eyes glistening with tears.

Arthur's gaze remained intently on ours, waiting for a response. I reached out to take his other hand, giving it a firm squeeze.

"We will," I said fervently. "I promise."

Those seemed to be the words he needed to hear to let go. The light went out in his eyes, and they permanently drifted shut.

13

ADRIFT

Our boat drifted further and further away from the *Demeter*. Rain no longer fell from the sky, and the fading rays of the sun painted the previously gray sky with shades of deep blue and violet. The stunning beauty of the waning day was a stark contrast to the horrors we'd just witnessed, as if nature itself wanted to wipe away the memory of those monstrosities.

I sat huddled next to Abe, my gaze sweeping from the *Demeter* to both Arthur and Lucy's dead bodies, which lay in the center of the boat. They both looked peaceful and serene, forever linked by death.

Abe was still as a statue, his eyes red with tears as he looked down at his friend's body. Seward continued to row, his eyes averted from Arthur and Lucy, his mouth set in a grim line.

"This . . . this is my fault," I said, my voice

breaking, as the sting of self-loathing began to stir beneath my grief. "I should not have convinced Arthur to come with us. This—it's my fight. I can continue on alone."

"Nonsense. No one is responsible for Arthur's death except for the creatures who slaughtered him," Abe bit out harshly. "Arthur insisted on facing them. He had to know he would not survive. It is my belief that he lost the will to live the moment we realized Lucy had been infected. He told me many times that he could not bear to live without her. When a man is determined to die . . . no one can stop him."

Though I believed Abe's words, my guilt and grief did not lessen, and I closed my eyes against a fresh wave of tears.

"How'd this happen? How was the ship overrun by those damned creatures? It happened so quickly," Seward spoke up, rattled. "When I woke up from my nap, Arthur and Lucy weren't in their cabin. Lucy must've gotten free and Arthur went after her. I went up to the deck and those things—they were swarming."

"The captain did mention ill crew members when we first boarded," Abe replied. "The shipmates must have already been in the final stages of the transformation—they were most likely infected at the same time."

"Infected shipmates on a cargo ship that makes regular stops in London? That seems too deliberate to be coincidental," I said, trying to focus my thoughts as I wiped away my tears.

"I agree," Abe said, somberly meeting my eyes. "I assume the captain logged every port where the ship has been docked in his journal. It could help us ascertain where the sailors were infected."

"Bloody hell," Seward whispered. "If *vampires* purposefully infected the shipmates..."

"Sailors are an ideal way to spread vampirism. They move from port to port, ship to ship. Think of all the great plagues that have hit Europe—many were spread across the continent by sea," Abe replied.

We fell darkly silent as the implication of his words settled in. I desperately wanted to be wrong about an invasion, but the evidence in its favor was increasing.

"The man who helped us on the *Demeter*," I said suddenly, recalling our mysterious savior. "He seemed... familiar, but I've never seen him before. He knew about vampires and how to kill them. Did either of you notice him? Recognize him?"

"No," Seward said regretfully. "Whoever he was, he helped save our lives."

Sorrow flickered through me as I returned my focus to the *Demeter*, now a small speck on the distant horizon. Our savior had no doubt perished on the ship.

"That ship will eventually arrive on some shore," Abe said, frowning as he followed my eyes.

"Those bodies are going to be found. There will be many questions."

"The authorities'll explain it away," Seward said bitterly. "I've seen it with the Ripper murders. *'A rogue wolf somehow got aboard and attacked the sailors, who were already ill with fever'*," he continued, taking on the authoritative tone of what I assumed was an inspector; it reminded me of the condescending Scotland Yard inspector at the Langham. "They won't come to the conclusion of vamp—vampires. I've seen the damn things and I can hardly even say the word."

"What do we do about Arthur and Lucy?" I asked. "If we alert the authorities to collect their bodies, there will be an inquest; questions we're not prepared to answer."

"We will bury them near the shore," Abe said, after a long pause, his eyes leaden with grief as he once again looked down at Arthur. "When this is all over, we can arrange to have their bodies returned to England. There is no evidence of our presence on the ship. I have Arthur and Lucy's bag. Arthur's friends and family were aware of Lucy's illness—he told them he would travel with her throughout the continent to see about doctors and would be away for a few weeks. That gives us some time. No one will be expecting them."

We nodded our agreement. Though I was uneasy at the thought of burying them in some random location, taking the time to fabricate a story about what happened to them for the local authorities would cause an even greater delay and ultimately be futile. Arthur's final request to destroy the vampire who had taken Jonathan was still fresh in my mind, and I fully intended to keep my promise to him without delay.

We soon spotted a shore in the near distance. Abe reached into his bag, unearthing a compass.

"From where the ship was last, that shore should be southern Holland. After . . . after we bury Arthur and Lucy," he said, with great difficulty. "We should find the nearest town and arrange for horses to a train station."

Our boat eventually drifted into shallow waters near the shore, and we all got out to help pull the boat the rest of the way onto the beach. I straightened and took in our surroundings. The beach we stood on curved and winded in both directions like an unfurled ribbon, edged by grassy dunes that gave way to more solid ground. In the near distance, I could see a small fishing village that hugged the shore.

Without speaking, we quickly and quietly moved into action. Abe and Seward carried both Arthur and Lucy's bodies out of the boat, and I directed them up the dunes to a grassy area of firm ground fifty yards away from the shore. We worked in silence, digging into the moist earth with our bare hands to create a wide, shallow burial area for the both of them. When we had a sizable space, I stood back as they gingerly deposited Arthur and Lucy inside. Together, we somberly buried them in the earth. When they were completely buried, I found nearby rocks and placed them over the makeshift grave.

We stood for a lengthy moment of silence over the grave. Though I had only known Arthur briefly, I could tell that he was a good man, and had loved his wife deeply. I recalled the brief look of love in Lucy's eyes right before she died, the helpless cries of the dying shipmates aboard the *Demeter*, our savior being pulled back onto the ship by the vampire, Arthur's anguished eyes right before he died. Beneath my sorrow, a surge of rage arose, hot and fierce. How many lives had those creatures taken? How many lives would they continue to take if they weren't stopped?

Soft weeping at my side pulled me from my angry reverie. Abe had pressed his face into his hands, his shoulders shaking with sobs. I was momentarily taken aback at the sight; Abe was a man who usually held control over his emotions. The last time I had seen him weep was at Father's funeral. At the time, my own grief had been so great that I'd barely been able to comfort him.

I turned him towards me. He dropped his hands, and I stepped into the circle of his arms, allowing him to bury his face in my hair and continue to weep. As Abe wept, Seward remained stoic, but I saw that his lips moved in silent prayer.

Abe composed himself and stepped back, giving me a nod of gratitude before he knelt down to place his hand over the grave.

"Goodbye Arthur, my friend. Goodbye Lucy," he whispered. "I–I am sorry that I failed you both."

He closed his eyes and murmured a silent prayer, tears spilling from behind his lids, before returning to his feet.

"We should head to that fishing village," he said, nothing in his tone betraying his outpouring of emotion only seconds earlier. Without waiting for a reply, he hoisted up the bags onto both shoulders, turning towards the dirt path that led away from the shore to the village. I watched him go with concern, knowing that he would bury his grief until it became a part of him. I had done the same with Father's death.

Seward trailed after him, shouldering his own bag, but I lingered for a moment longer at Arthur and Lucy's grave. *When the time is right, I will tell the world of your bravery. I promise that your deaths won't be in vain,* I vowed.

I joined Abe and Seward as they reached the path, and we continued towards the village, still stricken with mutual grief.

As we neared the outskirts of the fishing village, I could see the fishing boats that crowded the small harbor lined with cottages. A steepled church and town hall dominated the central square, surrounded by more homes and buildings that sprawled out from the square to line the narrow streets. It was a small village, with likely a minuscule population, but when we entered the central square, we saw no signs of life at all. The village looked as if it had been abandoned.

I saw a flicker of movement by the window of one of the cottages that edged the square, and twenty men suddenly raced out of the surrounding homes, armed with knives, scythes, and pickaxes, aiming them directly at our hearts.

We froze as a stocky man of medium height stepped forward, his grip firm on the hilt of a long knife. He wore the same traditional dress of the other men: baggy trousers, a long-sleeved shirt, wooden shoes, and a fisherman's hat. Like Captain Harper, he had the rough look of a man who was more accustomed to life at sea than on land. He seemed to be the de facto leader of the group; the other men fell back to watch him as he approached.

"*Wie ben jij? Waarom ben je hier?!*" he demanded.

I spoke some Dutch, but the man's words were spoken too quickly for me to understand. Abe held up his hands to indicate that we meant no harm, his tone strained but calm as he replied in Dutch.

"There was an accident on our ship, and we are stranded. We only need to borrow horses to get to the nearest train station," he said.

But the man continued to eye us suspiciously, and I could understand why. Our clothes were still damp from the storm and the sea, splattered with dirt and blood; our eyes shadowed with shock and fatigue. We looked as if we'd just stepped off a battlefield.

The other men began to shout at Abe in rapid Dutch, their voices rising with increased hostility. Abe replied to them in Dutch, but I could tell that he wasn't calming them down. I anxiously scanned the village, noticing a petite woman who hovered in the doorway of a small house next to the church. She wore a dark brown dress with an apron, her hair tucked beneath a cotton bonnet, her dark eyes wide with worry. In her hand, she clutched a wooden cross. Above her, several cloves of garlic hung above the doorway.

I stiffened when I saw the garlic, realizing the cause of their suspicions. Vampires. This village must have come under attack. It would explain its near abandoned state, and their excessive caution towards three unarmed strangers.

I turned to approach the woman. The men began to shout at me now, and I could feel the ire of their gazes as their attention turned towards me.

"Mina! What are you doing?" Abe shouted in English, panicked, before switching back to Dutch. "Please, she means you no harm!"

The woman met my eyes as I approached, and I saw alarm cross her features before the leader and his men hurriedly surrounded me, stopping me in my tracks. The leader's eyes were hard as they settled on me, and he stepped forward to press the blade of his knife against my heart. If I moved even slightly, it would pierce through the fabric of the dress to my skin.

"Please! She means you no harm!" Abe shouted again. His words did nothing to ease the suspicion in the man's look.

"She's not armed!" Seward shouted.

"*Alsjeblieft*," I implored him, in hesitant Dutch. I looked past the man at the woman, who continued to watch me with unease. "I see your garlic, your cross, your weapons. I know what you fear. *Bloedzuigers. Vampiers. Monsters.*"

The last word was the same in both English and Dutch, and the leader flinched with surprise at my words, while the woman stilled. The armed men exchanged astonished looks as well. My suspicions were correct.

I evenly met their eyes; nothing less than the truth would make them trust us.

"Vampires have attacked us as well. They killed our friends. They took over our ship, and now we're stranded; that's why we're covered in blood. And . . . they took someone I love. From London," I said, trying to keep my voice steady, but it shook as I thought of Jonathan. "We intend to rescue him, and kill the vampires who took him. We just need to borrow horses to continue on our journey. Believe that we understand your fear. But we are on the same side, and we truly mean you no harm."

For a long and strained moment, the man's gaze remained on my face, hard and resolute as stone, his knife still pressed against my heart.

"Gijs," the woman finally spoke, turning to look at the man. "Let her go."

14

IJSBRAN

I slipped out of my stained, damp dress and undergarments, dropping them in a heap on the floor before using the wash bin in front of me to carefully scrub the dried dirt and blood from my skin. I looked around the minuscule bedroom. Furnished only with a narrow bed, a layer of dust covered the floor and walls, and a musky scent hung in the air; it was clear that it had not been used in some time.

Just outside the window, I could hear the low murmur of conversation from Gijs, his wife Katrien —the woman whom I had approached—and a few of the other villagers.

Moments earlier, Gijs had apologized for their hostility after they all lowered their weapons.

"Been attacked many times by those beasts," he had said gruffly, in halting English. "Learned to be careful of strangers."

"Careful?" Seward demanded, furious. "You could've bloody killed us."

"Didn't know if you were one of those beasts," Gijs replied, his tone hardening. "Those monsters wear human skin."

"Gijs," Katrien spoke up. "They've been through much. Let them change clothes and take a meal . . . then we talk."

Gijs did not protest, and Katrien led us to two empty cottages on the edge of the square to wash and change into our spare clothes.

Now, I dried myself off before changing into a tan traveling dress and secured my loose hair back into a low bun before leaving the room. Abe and Seward had joined the others, and we trailed them to Gijs and Katrien's home.

In their sizable kitchen, Katrien provided us with a meal of bread, herring, and boiled potatoes. Several of the armed men who had surrounded us earlier also crowded inside the kitchen, their former suspicious hostility replaced by curiosity. They were joined by a few women, whom I suspected must have been hiding in other cottages during our approach. They were dressed similarly to Katrien, in simple dark dresses covered with aprons, white caps covering their hair.

As we began to eat, Abe gave them an overview of what happened on the *Demeter* and back in London. They listened intently, their faces filled with fright, but no one looked particularly surprised. When Abe finished, a brief silence fell before Gijs began to speak.

"Many families lived here," he said quietly. "They've fled."

"When did the attacks begin?" Seward asked.

Gijs responded in Dutch, speaking slowly enough for me to understand. Abe and I listened, and Abe periodically translated for Seward.

"A year ago. Heard stories about other villages in the countryside, but didn't think they were true until like things began to happen here. Men, women . . . sometimes entire families vanish from their homes in the night. Cattle and humans drained of blood. Men and women started to appear in the middle of the night, standing at the village edge, just watching us. Thought they were wandering vagrants or gypsies from the countryside —but they attacked and abducted villagers . . . and I knew they were beasts. Vampires."

My heart did an uneasy catapult, and I exchanged a dark look with Abe. How many stories like these had we heard in the Transylvanian countryside? How many had we dismissed?

"The last attack—" Gijs began, faltering at the memory. "I awoke and looked out to see many of those beasts in the streets. They . . . they pulled men out of their homes and took them away. Two beasts came in my home. I had Katrien and our two children hide in the cellar. I held up a cross, but it did nothing. They laughed, the beasts! They took my knife. I prayed they'd kill me, leave my family be. Didn't fight when they pounced on me."

"Gijs," Katrien whispered, tears spilling from her eyes at his words. Gijs placed his hand over hers, his eyes haunted. The other villagers were silent, their expressions matching Gijs', and I wondered how many of them had similar stories.

"You don't have to tell us, if it's too—" I began, but Gijs shook his head and continued.

"The beasts—they drank from me, but stopped feeding. Looked at me as if *I* were the monster. Grabbed their throats like they couldn't breathe, and fled. I was weak, and fainted. When I woke, they'd all gone."

"You were not infected in anyway? Or transformed?" Abe breathed, his gaze traveling over Gijs with medical scrutiny.

"No," Gijs replied, sounding amazed as he shook his head. "Days before, I played with my children in the wood. Came across a plant—we call it *monnikskap*; it's poison. Touched it with my bare skin. Katrien put together a *tegengif* before it could kill me."

I didn't recognize the word *tegengif*; Abe translated it as 'antidote' for me and Seward.

"Your blood still carried trace of this poison during the attack," I whispered, my mind racing. "That's what affected the vampires?"

"Yes. It saved my life," Gijs replied, solemn.

"*Monnikskap*," Abe said, closing his eyes,

before continuing in English, "Wolfsbane. Of course!"

"Wolfsbane?" Seward echoed with a puzzled frown.

"In Dutch, it is *monnikskap*. In English, wolfsbane. The scientific term is aconitum, or aconite—it has many names. It is a poisonous plant, especially deadly to wolves. I recorded it in my notes as a potential poison for vampires, and I started to experiment with it in my lab. But I did not dare test it on Lucy . . . not when I was trying to save her."

"It's how we've been able to remain here," Gijs said, his voice now filled with pride. "We sent our children to Amsterdam to live with Katrien's kin, and many others chose to flee. The rest of us take in the *monniksap* and antidote—it taints our blood for the beasts. Only one attack since then—no one died."

He seemed proud of this fact, but Abe frowned at him.

"You should not do that to yourselves. Ingesting poison—even in small amounts—will have a perilous long term effect on your bodies."

I closely studied Gijs, Katrien and the other villagers. I could now see that they all had an unhealthy pallor to their skin.

"We've no choice," Katrien said, her eyes still shining with tears, speaking in Dutch so rapidly that I had to concentrate to understand her. "We went to the police in Rotterdam . . . even Amsterdam. They think this is the fault of wolves or some illness—they think we are foolish villagers."

At her words, I was flushed with guilt, and again, Abe and I exchanged glances. We had once thought the same thing of the villagers in Transylvania.

I studied their resolute faces; the desperation paired with defiance in their eyes. I thought of the attack on the *Demeter,* the abductions in the Langham, and how helpless I had felt during both. How would I feel if my home were constantly suffering the same attacks, and no one believed me? I would be willing to do whatever it took to defend myself and fight back. But they couldn't poison themselves indefinitely. Soon it would take its toll on their bodies, and the vampires would take advantage. They would be slaughtered. Unless . . .

"Come with us," I said on impulse.

At my side, Abe stiffened, translating my words for Seward, who looked at me with quiet surprise. Gijs stilled, while Katrien and the others frowned.

"We fight the same evil. We want to fight with villagers like you who've been terrorized by those monsters. You must know that you can't keep poisoning yourselves," I continued.

But Gijs was unmoved by my words. "This village is home. My family has been here for years. I'll not leave it to the beasts." He turned to face his wife and the other villagers who stood around him. "You can go with them if you choose. I stay."

"I'll not leave you, *mijn geliefde*," Katrien whispered, grasping his hand.

The villagers exchanged glances. After a long silence, a tall stocky man with piercing steel grey eyes and graying red hair stepped forward.

"We stay," he pronounced. He seemed to speak for the others, as they all nodded in agreement. "Ijsbran is home."

Disappointment flooded through me as I took in their resolute faces. Having other villagers join us was a crucial part of our plan. Would other villagers we encountered along the way be just as determined to remain behind and defend their villages? If so, how could we even hope to take on such a massive threat alone?

Gijs was defiant as my eyes met his, as if daring me to challenge them. I gave him a nod to indicate that I understood.

"If any of you should change your minds—" Abe spoke up.

"We'll not," Katrien interrupted.

"If you do," Abe gently repeated. "I will leave behind my address in Amsterdam. Any messages you send there will be forwarded to me, wherever I am."

Gijs changed the subject, telling us that he knew the train schedule well. The nearest train station was in Rotterdam, from which the last train of the day had already departed. He offered us shelter for the night, and then transport to

Rotterdam the next morning in one of the village's fishing boats, which would be faster than traveling overland.

Abe politely began to ply them with questions about the village, and I could see Gijs and the others begin to relax. They must have thought that we'd continue to press them to join us or dissuade them from using the wolfsbane.

Gijs told us of the bustling fishing village that Ijsbran had once been, and the families that once lived here—many of whom had dwelled here for generations. His face darkened as he told us of the villagers who fled, their distress and pain at having to leave, something they did out of desperation rather than desire. Silence fell over the kitchen as he spoke of them, the shared woe on the faces of the villagers plain as they thought of their departed brethren—both alive and dead.

When we were finished with our meal, Katrien led us to the same two cottages that we had changed in. We would rest there for the night. We thanked her, and gathered in the minuscule kitchen of my cottage after she left us.

"I do not think we should depart from Paris as we originally planned," Abe said. "We should instead depart from Amsterdam—we will not lose much time; we can travel to Munich and continue on to Klausenburgh."

"We've already been delayed enough," I

protested. "Why do you want to depart from Amsterdam?"

"The aconite—wolfsbane. It could be a valuable weapon for us, but not the way the villagers are using it. While I have been away, my assistant has been researching ways of killing vampires en masse and sending me updates via telegram. The last one sent to me in London was quite promising, but I need to get my laboratory in person to assess the possible use of aconite as a weapon."

I hesitated. The attack on the *Demeter* had proven how unprepared we were to fight against a group of vampires, but I was reluctant to delay our journey yet again.

"Abe's right, Mina. You saw what happened on the *Demeter*. We lost one of our own and barely survived. How do you think we'll stand against fifty of those bloody things? More?" Seward asked.

"All right," I reluctantly replied. "But we leave from Amsterdam tomorrow."

"Of course," Abe said.

Seward and Abe left to retire to their cottage for the night, but Abe soon returned.

"I am leaving behind Arthur and Lucy's belongings. It is too cumbersome to keep carrying their bag. Lucy has dresses you may be able to wear."

I thanked him, though the thought of wearing the deceased woman's clothes seemed morbid. But

I had only brought three dresses with me, and already lost one.

"Abe—" I said hastily, stopping him before he could leave. "You can talk to me about Arthur at any time, if you feel the need. I know that he was your friend."

"Thank you, but I am all right," he said, not meeting my eyes as he gave me a forced smile. He turned and left before I could reply.

Before I settled in to bed, I packed two of Lucy's dresses that proved she had been a fashionable woman: a fine violet walking suit and a rose-colored dress made of silk brocade, along with two veiled hats adorned with satin ribbons.

When I crawled into bed, I held up my engagement ring, thinking of Jonathan as I gazed at the ruby stone. The more I learned about vampires and their attacks, the more I feared for him. Why had they taken him? Had they harmed him?

I awoke early the next morning after a fitful sleep. I washed and dressed, leaving the cottage to cross the village square towards Gijs and Katrien's home. Abe and Seward were already in the kitchen, seated opposite Gijs and some of the villagers, speaking in hushed tones over a breakfast of potatoes, bread and chicory, discussing the past attacks on the village. I frowned, irritated that I hadn't been awoken to join them, but Katrien intercepted me.

"I told them to let you sleep," Katrien said with a warm smile as she handed me a plate.

Breakfast was over quickly, and when we were finished eating, Gijs led us to the docks on the very edge of the village that hugged the shore.

A small fishing boat was waiting for us, but before we could board, Katrien presented Abe with a small pouch. He opened it to reveal at least a cluster of wolfsbane plants, securely nestled inside.

"I am grateful, but we cannot use this," Abe said immediately, handing the pouch back to Katrien. "It is too dangerous to travel with these as they are, and there are only three of us. You have far more need of—"

"Plant grows plentiful here," Gijs interrupted, reaching out to push the pouch back towards Abe.

I could tell that they would refuse to take it back, so I reached out to accept the pouch. Abe gave me a sharp look, but I smiled politely at Gijs and Katrien.

"Thank you. And thank you for all of your kindness." I said, tucking the pouch into my bag.

Katrien returned my smile, but her dark eyes were hard as granite, and she replied in English.

"Thank us by killing those beasts."

15

SYMBIOSIS

Gijs transported us to one of the many docks at Rotterdam's busy port. He bid us a solemn farewell, urging us to be careful.

We took a cab to a telegraph office, where we each sent wires. I sent a wire to Jonathan's boss Peter Hawkins, alerting him that Jonathan was missing if he wasn't aware, and inquiring about what he and Jonathan had discussed the night of the ball. Abe sent a wire to his lab assistant to let him know of our pending arrival and to relay instructions, while Seward wired both Scotland Yard and a police contact of his in Amsterdam. He told us he wanted to inquire about any similar incidents of murders or disappearances in Amsterdam that echoed the ones in London.

During the brief train ride from Rotterdam to Amsterdam, Abe was oddly quiet, his haunted gaze trained out of the window, likely thinking of Arthur. Across from us, Seward read through the captain's journal, raking his hand through his hair. I was consumed by thoughts of my own. I thought of Gijs, Katrien and the other villagers poisoning themselves to survive. How many other villages throughout Europe had suffered such attacks? What had they resorted to in order to survive?

I managed to set aside my worried thoughts when we arrived at the train station in Amsterdam. At my urging, we purchased train tickets for later that same day to Klausenburgh, with a connection through Munich.

We emerged from the station and quickly found a cab. As it clattered away, I took in the outskirts of the city, struck with a sudden rush of nostalgia. I had accompanied Father here when he attended lectures at the Royal Academy of Sciences, or gave guest lectures of his own at the Municipal University of Amsterdam.

But most of my memories of the city were linked with Abe. Though Abe had been born in Harleem, he spent most of his adult years in Amsterdam, and for me, the city had become synonymous with him.

While Father attended to his own matters, Abe would take me on long exploratory walks around the city, from Dam Square to the *Grachtengordel* neighborhood, where the myriad of canals built during the seventeenth century hinted at the city's

Golden Age. We had spent many hours in Vondel Park, either cycling along its paths or finding a quiet space to read. It was during one of our walks in the park where we first confessed our love for each other. We had initially decided to keep our courtship a secret from Father, uncertain as to how he would react, but planned to inform him of our engagement right before his final tragic trip. And though I ended our relationship after Father's death over my guilt, shock and grief, I greatly regretted that Father had never known of our love.

I glanced at Abe, wondering if he had been struck with similar memories, but his features were unreadable as he focused on the passing sights of the city.

Abe lived close to the train station, so we decided to stop briefly at his home for extra clothes, supplies and weapons before heading to our destinations.

"There are dresses in one of the guest rooms, should you need more," Abe informed me, when the cab stopped at his townhouse.

At his words, I felt an abrupt, surprising and completely inappropriate twinge of jealousy. I knew that Abe wasn't married—he would have mentioned such a thing. A mistress, perhaps? I doubted that as well. Even before Abe and I had begun courting, he had never seemed concerned with women; his only focus had been on his studies and research. But Abe was undeniably handsome; a well-educated man of the middle class, even if he would eschew such a distinction. I didn't expect him to remain unwed forever, especially when I myself was engaged, yet my chest still tightened at the thought.

Abe unlocked the door and led us inside. From the narrow entryway, I could see the drawing room from where I stood; it looked just as it had when I'd last been here.

There was no indication that anyone other than Abe lived here. The walls were mostly bare, the few items of wooden furniture simple. Like Father's study back home, every surface, including the floor, was practically brimming over with stacks of books and papers. I knew that Abe had a housekeeper come over on occasion, but he had once told me he hated his things being fussed over. He preferred a sort of organized chaos when it came to his belongings.

"I left in a bit of a haste," he apologized, following my eyes to the cluttered drawing room. "Seward, I have more knives in the cellar down the hall. Mina, do you remember where—"

"Yes," I interrupted, moving of my own accord up the stairs to the second floor, where I headed towards the guest bedroom at the end of the hall. It was a small room, dominated by the bed, wardrobe and central table, with a narrow window that looked out onto the street below. It was the room I stayed in when we visited Amsterdam. Here, I would read late into the night, waiting until Father fell asleep in his own guest room. Abe and I would then find each other, tucking ourselves away in the drawing room or slipping outside, where we would walk hand in hand along the canals. How happy I had been in those days, unaware of the darkness that lie ahead.

A shimmer of tears clouded my eyes. I blinked them back, overwhelmed by all the memories the city had inadvertently brought to the surface, and made my way to the wardrobe.

I froze in astonishment when I opened it, finding several of my traveling dresses and cloaks folded inside. We had visited here so often that I had begun to leave clothes here. With the suddenness of Father's death and subsequent end of my relationship with Abe, I had forgotten that they were even here. Why had Abe never gotten rid of them or sent them to me?

The question was still on my mind as I changed into a brown traveling dress and hat that fit as well as I remembered, and carefully folded one more into my bag, leaving Lucy's finer dresses behind.

Abe and Seward were waiting for me in the entrance hall as I descended the stairs. Noticing the dress I wore, Abe avoided my eyes and asked if I was ready to go, to which I gave him an abrupt nod. Seward studied us with curiosity. Perceptive as always, he had picked up on the slight tension between us.

When we made our way down Abe's quiet residential street to flag down cabs, I felt it. The now familiar and chilling sensation of a cold gaze on the back of my neck.

I whirled, frantically looking around, but the street around us was empty. Abe and Seward stopped mid-stride, looking back at me with puzzled frowns. I took another look around the empty street before meeting their eyes. I could no longer dismiss this.

"For the past week, I've sensed someone watching me. Back in London at my parents' graves, then at Tilbury Docks right before we boarded the *Demeter*. And just now," I concluded.

Abe stiffened at my words, turning to scan the empty street, while Seward looked cautious.

"You are certain?" he asked.

"Yes. The vampire who took Jonathan at the Langham . . . he looked right at me, and I felt the same chill. The—the same chill I felt the night Father was murdered, when that creature looked at me."

"Was the sensation of being watched cold? A sort of frost on your skin?" Abe asked.

"Yes," I replied, surprised by his accuracy.

"I have felt a similar sensation," Abe said, answering my silent question. "The night Robert was killed, the ball, the docks, and just now."

"Why didn't you say anything before?" I asked, stunned.

"I thought I was being unnecessarily apprehensive—paranoid," Abe said. "But if you have sensed it as well..."

Seward now looked alarmed, straightening to search the street around us.

"I've not noticed anything. You think... you think one of those things are following us?" he asked. "How come we haven't been attacked? It's had plenty of opportunity."

"I don't know. But after all that's happened, I doubt it's a mere coincidence," I replied.

"We will just have to remain vigilant," Abe said, with firm resolve. "Are you both armed?"

I nodded, my hand instinctively going to my bag, where I had stored my kukri knives. Seward nodded as well, indicating the revolver beneath his jacket.

After another cautious look around, we continued towards the busy street of Haarlemmerstrat. We took separate cabs, agreeing to meet at the train station at half past five. But as our cab transported me and Abe to the Municipal University of Amsterdam, I was still filled with anxiety over who —or what—was following us, and I continually scanned the streets around us. When the cab dropped us at the university, fear continued to simmer beneath my awareness, and I barely took in my surroundings as Abe led me into one of the baroque-style buildings, down a corridor and into a large empty classroom.

A pretty young woman with delicate features and flaxen blonde hair haphazardly tucked into a bun was seated at one of the desks, furiously writing down notes in a journal, deep in concentration. She straightened when she noticed us standing at the doorway.

"Your assistant?" I asked, turning to face Abe with a frown. "Where is he?"

"He," Abe said, sounding amused, "is standing right in front of you."

The young woman set down her journal and nervously stepped forward.

"Mina, this is Greta Steinder, my research assistant. Greta, this is Mina Murray," Abe said politely, still looking amused by my quiet astonishment.

"Mina! I mean, Miss Murray. I heard much of you . . . and your father. Doctor Van Helsing gave me some of your father's work to read. I must have read his paper on comparative anatomy in vertebrates four times. It is such a pleasure to make your acquaintance," Greta said.

I felt an instant warmth towards her that replaced my surprise. It was the first time since his death that I'd met someone who hadn't disparaged my father and complimented his work.

"I'm pleased to meet you as well," I said, smiling. "And please, call me Mina."

"Your wire seemed urgent, Doctor Van Helsing," Greta said, returning my smile before looking at Abe with concern.

"Much has happened," Abe replied, expelling a sigh. "I am afraid we do not have much time. We are on our way to Transylvania. We depart later today. I will try to explain as much as I can, but I need to know what you have discovered during my absence."

"Transylvania?" Greta echoed, her brown eyes going wide, and I could tell that she had many questions. But she seemed to understand our urgency, and turned to head out of the classroom, gesturing for us to follow. "Please come with me."

While we made our way down the corridor, Abe told her what he had observed in London, the abductions at the Langham, our experiences on the *Demeter*, and the villagers who took us in. She went pale as she listened, and turned to give me a look of genuine sympathy when Abe mentioned Jonathan's abduction.

She stopped at a set of double doors at the end of the corridor, unlocking them and stepping inside. Abe and I trailed her inside.

It looked more like a zoo than a lab, filled to the brim with cages containing various small animals—minks, martens, voles, badgers.

I studied the animals, stiffening with dread. Even in animals I could recognize the effects of vampirism, with their abnormally sharp teeth and unnaturally colored eyes of either black or red.

"These animals were roaming the countryside," Abe said, stepping around Greta to enter the lab further, examining the animals with a critical eye. "Greta discovered many of them on her own, and she brought them in."

Abe moved towards a caged badger, gesturing for me to come closer. It growled as I neared, and I moved towards it with great hesitation.

"Do you see these two prick marks?" Abe asked, pointing towards two large pin-like holes in the badger's throat area. "They are similar to marks we have seen on human bodies drained of blood."

I studied the badger's wound, before turning to study the other animals. They all bore similar marks.

"For some vampires, especially new ones, it may be easier to hunt and feed on animals than humans," Abe said. "In our observations, vampirism acts more like a disease in animals than as a transformative property as it does in humans. Though there are some transformative traits. As you can see, they behave as if they have been infected by a particularly virulent form of rabies. They become increasingly aggressive, and they reject all food but the blood of other animals."

"How is it spread among animals?" I asked, dreading the answer.

"It appears to simply be contagious. One

infected animal drains another of its blood. If that animal survives, it displays similar vampiric traits. Not all animals become infected, but many do. The effect seems to vary—as it does in humans."

"Can they infect humans as well?" I asked.

"Greta?" Abe asked, and I started for a moment. I had been so focused on what he was telling me that I'd nearly forgotten Greta was there, silently hovering behind us. "Would you like to answer this one?"

Greta nodded, flushing at our renewed attention on her. "No, they cannot. I was bitten while handling two of the martens, but other than smarting a bit, I was fine. Their bites seem to only work on other animals."

A flicker of relief went through me. I did not want to learn of another source of vampirism in nature.

"You mentioned in your wire you have made a discovery?" Abe asked.

"Yes," Greta replied. "Several days ago, one of the martens escaped from its cage and killed the animal that infected it. Once that animal died, the ones he infected were cleared of their vampiric traits, and they returned to their pre-infected states. I've been observing them, and they remain free of vampirism."

As she spoke, she led us to a row of cages in the back of the lab that contained even more badgers and martens. Unlike the other animals, they appeared completely docile and ... natural. I found it hard to believe that they had been infected at all.

"Killing the host cured the animals it infected. It's just as you've theorized about vampirism being a biologically symbiotic relationship, Doctor Van Helsing," Greta continued, her voice rising with eagerness. "The host is linked to the one it creates. Once the host dies, the link is broken and the infection cured."

I recalled Lucy's strange symbiotic link with the vampire who transformed her. A symbiotic relationship made sense.

"A cure," I whispered, filled with a sudden rush of hope. If Jonathan had been bitten and transformed, it would be possible to cure him if we killed the one who turned him.

"There are some caveats," Greta quickly added. "We don't know if the effect will be the same in humans and vampires. Even if it is, the host needs to be killed quickly after infection. The infected animals who were cured had been infected within the past week. Others who had been infected for many weeks remained so."

"Greta, your discovery is still very impressive. Well done," Abe said, giving her a look of admiration. At his compliment, Greta flushed once more and nodded her thanks. Though I could tell their relationship did not go beyond the boundaries of student and professor, a small stab of jealousy pierced me at the exchange.

"This is a natural extension of what we have theorized, and what you proposed back on the *Demeter,* Mina," Abe said, turning back to me.

"Then we must get to Jonathan immediately," I said, my hope slowly becoming panic. "If he's already been bitten or transformed by those monsters—"

"We do not know that," Abe said gently, before turning back to Greta. "In my wire, I requested capsules of aconite. Were you able to procure them from Professor Christison in the medical school?"

"Yes. I told him it was for an experiment. He didn't question me too much," she said, giving him a reassuring smile before moving over to the far corner of the lab, where she opened a desk drawer and unearthed a small box. She handed it to Abe, and he opened it, examining the capsules inside for several long moments.

"I'm going to ask you to do something," he said suddenly, looking back up at Greta. "It falls beyond your duties as my laboratory assistant. If you do not want to do it, then please—"

"No," Greta said, pulling herself up to her full height, as if she were a soldier reporting for battle. "I want to help."

Abe moved to the doors and closed them.

"I need you to contact a gunsmith friend of mine, Johan Derichs. He also makes other weapons. He has a shop near Nieuwmarkt. Tell him I need multiple wooden stakes constructed and shipped to me in Klausenburgh, immediately. Mina, we can douse the stakes with the aconite. Hopefully, they will do great damage to any vampires we encounter. If he inquires what they are for, tell him I am traveling to a rural area in the eastern countryside overrun with rabid wolves, and the stakes are for personal defense," Abe continued.

I doubted that explanation would satisfy the gunsmith's curiosity, but I kept silent. Greta did not look surprised or uneasy by the request, and promised to contact him as soon as we left. When Abe stepped aside to write out detailed instructions for the gunsmith, I asked her how she came to know about vampires and work with Abe.

Her tale was similar to the villagers of Ijsbran. She was from a village that suffered from mysterious disappearances, strange people appearing in the night, cattle drained of blood, and then a final attack in which her grandparents were killed.

"I heard rumors of Doctor Van Helsing investigating the alleged 'wolf attacks'. I came to see him. I told him that based on the evidence, I didn't think they were wolf attacks at all. He was the only one to believe me," she said, her eyes glistening with tears.

Abe stopped writing and met her eyes with concern. She gave him a quick nod to indicate that she was all right, but I reached out to place my hand over hers. I knew the gesture was far too intimate for someone I had just met, but I felt a strong solidarity with her. She had also lost loved ones to those monsters.

Greta gave me a grateful smile as I removed my hand, moving to a long desk against the wall to pick up a small stack of journals and books.

"Here is the research you asked for," she said, stepping forward to hand them to Abe. "I've also included notes on my experiments with the infected animals."

"Thank you, Greta. You have been more helpful than you can ever realize. I will be in touch as much as I can during my travels," Abe said.

"Miss Mur—Mina," Greta corrected herself, as we made our way to the door, her eyes wide with worry. "Doctor Van Helsing. Whatever is happening . . . it frightens me. Please be careful."

16

PURSUED

When we met Seward at the train station, he informed us that dozens of men from several tenement buildings had been reported missing to the police. It proved what we already knew—that the abductions were also occurring here and in other European cities, but my heart still plummeted with dread at the news.

"News of the *Demeter*," Seward added, handing us a folded up newspaper. "It ran aground in northern England last night."

Abe took the newspaper, briefly scanning the headline and article, before handing it to me with a frown. The headline screamed:

TRAGEDY ABOARD THE DEMETER!

The brief article that followed mentioned the bodies of the crew and its captain, who appeared to have perished from a combination of a mysterious fever and some sort of wolf attack, as there were many bites found on the bodies. No animals were found aboard the ship. The assumption was made that the wolf had made its way on land once the ship ran aground, and all nearby residents should take caution. The police and coroner were still investigating.

"It's as I predicted. Some excuse to explain what can't be explained," Seward said with a heavy sigh. "I read through the captain's journal. He mentioned his men acting oddly before they fell ill, and he noted the ship's stops—several at a port in Varna. Varna's not far from Transylvania. There're many brothels in Varna. I've an uncle who's a sailor," he added, with a defensive flush at our raised eyebrows. "He and the other sailors would . . . entertain themselves there when they docked. A brothel's a good place to infect a group of sailors."

We fell silent at his words. If Seward was right, how many other sailors had been transformed? Were other ships filled with sailors on the verge of transformation?

Our somber silence persisted as we boarded the train, finding seats in a compartment near the rear. When the train pulled away from the station, I looked around at the other passengers. There was a young couple seated opposite us, their heads bent closely together, their hands subtly entwined in their laps, likely off to a honeymoon or some sort of romantic sojourn together. Behind them, an austere-looking businessman had his face buried in his newspaper, his lips silently moving as he read. A harried young mother chased her boisterous young son down the aisle; she quickly caught up to him, taking his hand and leading him to the back of the train. They were all caught up in their own trivial matters, unaware of the threat of vampires, and I was suddenly envious of their ignorance. Only days ago my largest concern had been dealing with Horace's snobbery and trying to win Mary's favor.

At my side, Abe took out Arthur's map of Transylvania and spread it out on his lap. Our planned route was encircled, and a large mark indicated our destination. The fortress nestled in the midst of the Carpathians.

"I had Greta gather some information from the university library about fortresses in the region. There is one in particular that matches what we are looking for—Napoeri Castle. It is massive and rather isolated. An ideal place to serve as a prison and build an army. It was built in medieval times and seems to have fallen into disuse a century ago. Many noble families once resided in its walls: the Bathorys, the Draculesti, the Skalas . . . perhaps the one we are looking for is connected to one of these families. We can try to find out more from the locals as we get closer. When we arrive in Klausenburgh, it should take a day or two of riding with stops before we arrive at the fortress—there are several villages we will pass along the way. It is quite likely that they have been attacked by these creatures. We can rally them to join us if they are willing."

"If there's anyone left," Seward added. At our sharp looks, he held up his hands defensively. "It's something to consider. Look at how empty Ijsbran was. If villagers in Transylvania have been attacked for years, why would they stay?"

"Pride. Look at how determined Gijs and the others were to defend their village. There must be others like them," I said, though I was trying to convince myself more than Seward.

Seward nodded, but he did not look entirely convinced. He excused himself to head to the smoking compartment, leaving us alone. Once he'd left, I looked back down at the map. What if Seward was right, and the majority of villagers had fled?

"If only we'd believed the villagers when they first told us of all this," I whispered, speaking my regret out loud for the first time. "Perhaps then Father would still be alive. Same with Arthur, Lucy, and countless others. I should have listened to you."

"Roads like that are endless if you let yourself travel them," Abe replied. "Even if we had believed the villagers then, no one else would have believed us, as we have seen. We would still be powerless, and the same events would have unfolded. Arthur would still be . . ." His voice wavered, and he fell silent for a moment before continuing, "It is my belief that we had to be forced to embark on this journey."

"I keep thinking about Father's missing journal," I confessed. "I know that he did not take it with him on his final trip—it wasn't with his other belongings. And his journal entries in the year prior to his death are not as detailed. I think he was purposefully leaving something out."

"I noticed it as well. Such brevity was not like him at all. It is fair to assume that he was hiding his observations about vampires. He was a Cambridge professor and a respected scientist. If word got out that he was treating creatures of folklore as legitimate science . . ."

"His scientific reputation was ruined anyway," I murmured, unable to keep the bitterness from my voice.

"There are those who know otherwise," Abe said reassuringly. "He was a brilliant man. Many respected him, regardless of how he died."

He refolded the map, tucking it away in his bag.

"Remember when we first arrived at that village in the foothills of the Carpathians? We observed a pair of lynxes from afar. Robert's excitement was so great, it was as if he had discovered the species himself."

I could tell that Abe was purposefully changing the subject, attempting to inject some levity into our dark conversation. But I went along with the shift, smiling at the memory.

"Of course," I replied. "He kept whispering that lynxes had been extinct in England for thousands of years. He never thought he'd see one. I think he was cross with us for not sharing his excitement."

It was a relief to discuss something other than vampires and their looming threat, and we began to trade stories of our research travels with Father. The Alps to observe herds of chamois; the shores of England to study aquatic animals of the North Sea; rural France to document rare species of insects in its forests. Abe made no mention of our secret courtship or engagement, but it was beneath the surface of every memory and every story, and I had to actively push those particular memories to the back of my mind.

"I must confess, there is something I cannot envision," Abe said, during a brief lull.

"What?" I asked.

"You becoming a Harker and officially joining London society. Having afternoon tea, arranging dinner parties. Becoming a matriarch like Mary Harker. Do you know that you looked perfectly miserable at the ball while trying to appear happy? I know your forced smiles exceedingly well," Abe said, looking mildly amused as he studied me. "I am not saying you do not love Jonathan," he added at my affronted expression. "Our journey proves how much you do. It . . . it is just not the life I envisioned for you."

The lightness I had just felt quickly vanished, and my body went rigid with defensive tension. His statements echoed the anxieties I already had about marrying Jonathan, but I didn't want him to know how accurate his musings were.

"Jonathan's life will be my life," I said, turning away from his perceptive gaze. "It will bring me great joy to become his wife. I certainly couldn't have wandered around Europe conducting experiments forever. Eventually, I was going to have to settle down."

"We planned to never settle," Abe said, his voice so low that I had to strain to hear him. "Remember?"

I said nothing, but I did remember. Our future was to be dedicated to both travel and research in Father's field of comparative anatomy —a field we both found immensely fascinating. We were to conduct experiments all over the world and jointly publish our findings. But that was before.

After Father's death, I had been so stricken that the thought of resuming my travels and scientific pursuits was too devastating, even with Abe at my side. The life that I had built for myself in London was safe. A refuge. I just wanted to return to it with Jonathan.

"I'm content with my life back in London," I said. "I just want to bring Jonathan home."

"Content?" Abe pressed.

"Abe—" I began, exasperated.

"All I want is your happiness, Mina. That is all I have ever wanted. But I will say nothing more about the matter," Abe said, looking away from me.

Seward soon returned, reeking heavily of tobacco, and we passed the time in silence as the train made its way further and further away from Amsterdam, and then south through the German countryside. I tried to read through Greta's research, but Abe's words dominated my thoughts, and I was unable to concentrate.

I excused myself to head to the smoking compartment, and I sensed Abe's eyes on me as I walked away. I hated the smell of tobacco, but I was restless and needed to move around.

The smoking compartment was empty when I entered. I remained standing to look out of the windows at the passing countryside. Night had fallen, and the trees outside looked like menacing shadows as the train hurtled past.

I felt a presence in the compartment behind me, and turned to see Seward enter, his focus also on the passing countryside. He made no move to smoke, which I suspected was for my benefit, and we stood in companionable silence for a lengthy stretch of time.

"I was born on a farm outside of London. There are times when I miss it—the countryside," he said finally, his eyes wistfully lingering on a farm as we passed it by. "But I hated it when I was a boy. I just wanted to live in London. My father thought I'd become a farmer like him. I–I still thought he'd be proud when I joined Scotland Yard. When I told my parents, he just said nothing, and my mother wept like a baby. I think they still hope I'll change my mind and go back to the farm. With what I've seen . . . that doesn't seem like such a mad prospect," he added gruffly. He tried to give me a light smile, but it was somewhat pained.

"What we've learned is indeed terrifying," I said. "I think that's why I was in denial for so long about what was happening. I didn't want to believe it. Thank you for joining us, Seward," I added impulsively. "I should have thanked you before. I'm glad you are with us."

"I just want to stop these bloody—" he began, abruptly stopping himself. "I'm sorry about the swearing, Mina. I keep forgetting you're a woman," he said, and then flushed. "Ah . . . I meant—"

"It's quite all right," I said. "You can swear around me, I won't disintegrate. Bloody hell, Jesus Christ, devil, damn. There. I'm still standing."

Seward looked both astonished and impressed by the oaths, blinking, his eyes wide. I couldn't stop the smile that curved my lips at the look on his face. This was a man who had seen gruesome dead bodies and vampires feasting on humans, yet the sight of a lady swearing left him stupefied. Seward sheepishly returned my smile, as if reading my thoughts.

"I'll keep that in mind," he said. "My intentions were selfish when I first joined the Ripper investigation," he continued, looking serious now. "I wanted to be the one to solve it and get promoted to first class inspector. Maybe I'm still that boy who wants to make his father proud. Then I saw the murder victims up close . . ." he trailed off, his face going pale at the memory.

"What made you think the killer wasn't human?" I asked, lowering my voice, though we were the only ones in the compartment.

"The way the bodies were drained of blood; the way the killer could just disappear. It seemed impossible to be the work of one—or even several—men. I contacted Abe not long after I had the first suspicions. He's a bit mad himself," Seward said, his mouth twitching with the beginnings of a smile. "My police contact in Amsterdam introduced us years ago when Abe consulted on a case. Abe's always willing to believe the impossible—the mark of a true scientist."

As I returned his smile, I froze. I once again felt the terrible and familiar sensation of cold eyes on my skin. I turned away from Seward, stepping forward to scan the carriage beyond the smoking compartment, but there was nothing amiss, and I saw no one looking at us.

"What?" Seward asked.

"I sensed it again," I whispered. "There's a vampire on the train with us."

"How DO we search the train for a vampire?" Seward whispered, in a low hiss.

We had just returned to our seats to inform Abe what I'd sensed. Abe immediately set down his journal, his hand straying to his coat pocket, where I suspected he had stored his weapon.

"They look human, don't they? It's how he's been able to follow us." Seward continued, darting a quick glance around at the other passengers, as if to illustrate his point.

"Even if we could identify the creature, we need to be careful," Abe whispered. "We do not want to force a confrontation, not with so many bystanders. When we stop in Munich, instead of switching trains, perhaps we can draw him out— somewhere safe and isolated. We can take a later train."

"No," I objected. "We've already been delayed enough. If the creature wanted to harm us, it would have happened by now. We'll have to act like nothing's amiss, and then force a confrontation when we arrive in Klausenburgh. That way we don't lose any time."

"You both assume he doesn't want to harm us," Seward argued. "And how do we know there's only one?"

"Even more reason for us to not force a confrontation here," I said, though I felt a shiver of apprehension at the thought of more than one vampire pursuing us. "We don't want to risk innocent people being harmed."

We agreed to stay close together until the train arrived in Klausenburgh, and to keep our weapons close at hand. Once we disembarked and picked up the shipment of stakes, we would ride out of the city as planned, allowing the creature to follow us until we could surround him.

When our train arrived at the Munich train station, we tried to keep up the guise that we were unaware of being followed. I subtly studied each passenger as we changed trains, but they all seemed innocuous and most importantly—human.

I was still on edge when our train departed Munich, wondering why we were being followed, and why the creature had not attacked us yet. Was he waiting for the perfect moment to strike? Was it a mistake to try and confront him in an isolated area?

I forced myself to concentrate on reading through Father's journal and Greta's research notes. When I glanced up sometime later, I saw that Abe had somehow managed to fall asleep, his head resting against the window, his wavy hair falling messily over his forehead as he dozed, his coat spread out on his lap. Abe was a man who lived very much in his mind, and it seemed that the only time his mind was at rest was when he slept. He had once angrily told me that he lost hours of thinking time when he slept, and I smiled at the memory.

Without thinking, I leaned forward to tuck his coat around him as a makeshift blanket, something I did many times on our previous travels together. The intimacy of the gesture didn't cross my mind until I found Seward studying me closely. I dropped my hands back into my lap, as if I had been caught stealing, and got to my feet.

"I'm going to use the lavatory," I mumbled. At his concerned frown, I gestured towards my sleeve to indicate that I was armed with my kukri.

I made my way to the lavatory at the rear of the train, nearly colliding with a man who stood up from his seat. I looked up to apologize, but the words died on my lips.

I recognized him. It was the mysterious man who had rescued us on the *Demeter*. He was dressed like a traveling businessman, donning a bowler hat and frock coat. His silver eyes flashed with urgency as he looked down at me.

"What—" I began, astonished.

"You and your friends need to get off this train,"

he interrupted. "*Now*."

"What are—"

The wheels of the train began to emit a sharp squeal as it slowed down in speed, cutting off my sentence. I dimly realized that the conductor was trying to stop the train.

"Get to the ground!" the man shouted, as the squealing increased to a great wail, and the walls of the train around us began to rattle.

The train violently lurched to the side, and I was thrown to the ground by the force. All around me, passengers screamed and cried out in alarm.

"Find something to hold onto!" the man shouted to both me and the hysterical passengers, reaching out to brace his body on the wall behind him.

Dazed and horrified, I remained on the ground, reaching out to grip the wall behind me, silently praying that Abe and Seward had taken cover. The carriage began to tilt as the train careened on to its side, the wheels now letting out an ear-splitting howl.

"Hold on, Mina!" the man shouted. "Hold on!"

I barely registered my confusion at the man knowing my name; I was too overcome by panic.

The train was about to derail.

I continued to hold on to the wall behind me as the train began to veer off the tracks, and the sounds of screams, cries and screeching tires soon faded into silence.

17

MASSACRE

I awoke to the smell of acrid flames and blood.

Disoriented, I blinked up at the wide expanse of night sky, my mind temporarily blank. As pained cries began to punctuate the stillness around me, my memories returned with a sudden grim clarity. The mysterious man's warning. The wheels squealing on the tracks. The keening howl of crushing steel as the train turned on to its side.

I sat up, crying out at the sharp pain that pierced my lower back as I moved. Wincing, I looked around. We were deep in the countryside, and the now gnarled and twisted train tracks were surrounded on both sides by thick forest.

Dozens of wounded or dead passengers were strewn all around me. I had been thrown several yards from the train, which mostly lay on its side like a mortally wounded animal. Half of the carriages were completely crumpled and destroyed.

The surviving passengers looked dazed, numb and horrified. I recognized some of them. The austere businessman, who now lay still on his back several yards away from me, his face streaked with blood. The mother and son, who sat next to the gnarled train tracks, the mother rocking her son, who was sobbing into her bosom, her face pale with shock. The young couple sat next to them; the woman had her paramour's head in her lap, sobbing. He lay stock still, his open eyes unseeing, blood soaking his shirt.

As I emerged from my shock, I became chillingly certain that this had been no accident. We were not safe here.

Grimacing, I forced myself to my feet. My entire body was sore and bruised, my left shoulder and lower back were badly sprained, but that appeared to be the extent of my injuries. I had to find Abe and Seward; we had to somehow get these people to safety.

"Mina..."

I turned to find the same man who had warned me on the train limping towards me. There was a deep gash etched into the side of his angular jaw, and he looked abjectly relieved to see me. I took a jerky step back at his approach. Though I'd thought that it was a vampire who had been following us, I knew that this man was our mysterious pursuer.

"You . . . you knew this was going to happen," I whispered. "You've been following us."

"Yes," he said, without hesitation. "I'm Gabriel. There's no time for me to explain who I am. I don't know how long it will take for help to arrive, but no one's safe here. Come."

I had no doubt of the truth of his words, but I still hesitated, not quite trusting him. I saw a flicker of impatience in his eyes as he stepped forward, lowering his voice.

"The train derailment was caused by vampires," he said bluntly. "They were the ones to twist these tracks. Believe me, they are very near. We must get everyone away from here. Your friends are on the other side of the tracks. One of them is injured."

He turned and limped away without waiting for my response. Though I was still vaguely suspicious of him and his knowledge of vampires, my concern for Abe and Seward outweighed it. I hurried after him, ignoring the sharp ache in my back and shoulder as I moved, and we made our way through the disoriented passengers who stumbled about the wreckage.

Further ahead, just on the edge of the forest, I spotted Abe and Seward. Seward had Abe propped against a tree, and Abe was eerily still.

At the sight of him, my fear turned to full-fledged panic and I broke into a run, the pain in my bruised body forgotten as I reached them, sinking to my knees opposite Abe.

A piece of shrapnel was embedded into Abe's side, and I pressed my hands to my mouth to stifle a strangled sob when I saw how much blood seeped from his wound, and how still and pale he was. I was taken back to the night I found Father, still and silent, lying in a pool of his own blood. *Not again*, I screamed in my mind. *Not Abe*.

Seward was speaking, but my agitation was so great that I couldn't make out his words. Ignoring him, I reached out a trembling hand towards Abe's throat to feel for a pulse.

My hand froze in mid-air. I could not bear to confirm for certain that he was dead, that I had lost another man I loved. I closed my eyes. Unable to quell my grief, I pressed my hand to my mouth as I began to weep.

A hand covered mine, and I almost yanked it away, assuming that it was Seward's.

"I am not quite dead yet, Mina."

The voice was raspy and weak, and my eyes flew open. Abe's blue eyes were partially open now, focused on me, and though I could tell he was in pain, he gave me one of his easy smiles. The enormous weight of grief lifted from my shoulders; my relief so immense that I nearly began to weep again. I leaned forward to place my hands on his face, my eyes still wet with tears, unable to form any words, still shaken by the possibility of losing him.

"We need to get something for your wound, and then we need to get everyone out of here," Gabriel said, his words forcing me back to the present. Abe's eyes lifted from mine to focus on Gabriel, recognition in his eyes.

"You . . . you were on the *Demeter*," Seward said, frowning at Gabriel in confusion.

"I'll explain who I am later. There are abandoned farmhouses just east of here. We can take able-bodied passengers with us to get help, but we must move quickly," Gabriel said.

"But Abe's wound . . . we need to remove the shrapnel," I said, looking down at the shrapnel still lodged in Abe's side.

"No. It needs to stay in. It is holding the wound together," Abe said, speaking with difficulty. "If you pull it out, I could very well bleed to death. I would need some sort of tourniquet to prevent that from happening."

"Then we need to—" Seward began.

"Quiet," Gabriel said abruptly, getting to his feet and scanning the surrounding trees. His entire body went rigid, his skin draining of color.

"What? What is it?" I asked.

"It's too late," he said, briefly closing his eyes.

I looked at him, dread tearing through my body. I knew who he was referring to. What he was referring to. And I could tell by Abe and Seward's panicked features that they also knew. I thought of the catastrophe on the *Demeter* and the abductions at the Langham as I took in the frightened and wounded passengers around us. It would be a massacre.

"Leave me," Abe rasped, meeting my eyes. "Take as many people with you as you can. I will not be—"

"Stop it. You know I'm not leaving you," I said, glaring at him. "We'll find another way. If we must, we can fight. I have my kukri on me, and your knives are still on the train. If our carriage wasn't destroyed, then—"

"Do you have the wolfsbane?" Gabriel asked. Seward, Abe and I looked at him, startled, and I once again felt a tingling suspicion. How did he know we had wolfsbane? "Do you?" he repeated, impatient.

"Yes," Seward replied.

"You won't be able to fight them off. Your weapons—even your wolfsbane—won't be enough to hold off a group of vampires this size. You need to get your weapons and move as quickly as you can in that direction," he said, pointing south through the trees. "There are some farmhouses a couple of kilometers away. You should be able to find bandages for Doctor Van Helsing's wounds there, but make sure you find a place to hide, and don't attempt to leave until I come for you. Leave."

"What about these people?" Seward asked,

gesturing to the helpless passengers around us. "We can't—"

"I'll do what I can for them. Leave," Gabriel repeated, already moving away from us.

We watched in dazed amazement as Gabriel raced towards the nearest group of passengers, kneeling down to speak urgently to them. How did he know so much about vampires? About us? Who was he?

"Mina, he's right. We need to go," Seward said. "Abe, can you walk?"

"Yes," Abe said with difficulty.

"Seward, help Abe up and head south. You have the strength to carry much of his weight," I said, forcing myself to focus. "I'll fetch our bags from our carriage."

"No," Abe protested weakly, shaking his head. "We will wait for you before we depart. If the vampires are almost upon us—"

"I'll be right behind you," I said, giving Abe a reassuring smile, though a sliver of trepidation crawled up my spine. "You're injured. We need to get you to safety first."

I leaned forward to touch the side of his face, holding his gaze. There were a multitude of things I wanted to say, but I focused on my most immediate and greatest desire.

"Stay alive," I whispered.

Before even more tears could threaten my thin grip on control, I turned and hurried towards the destroyed train. Out of the corner of my eye, I saw Gabriel moving quickly between the various groups of passengers. As he spoke to them, they each moved off into a different direction. *He's scattering them*, I realized. They had a better chance of survival if they were spread out, rather than being centered in a single location. I felt a small glint of admiration for Gabriel, whoever he was.

I approached the destroyed train, counting out the carriages until I spotted our own, which had been the third from the rear. My memory was correct and it was intact, resting askew on the tracks.

I made my way to the entrance, where the door to the carriage hung limply off its side. With great effort, and ignoring the steady throb of pain in my lower back, I stepped inside. Many of the seats were still in place, while multiple bags and shattered glass from the windows covered the interior of the carriage. I made my way towards the rear, scanning the various bags, until I spotted our bags, lodged beneath one of the seats. I hurried forward until I reached them, and reached into mine, taking out my additional kukri and the pouch of wolfsbane. I tucked the wolfsbane into the bodice of my dress and the kukri into my other sleeve. I had just begun to knot the straps of our bags around my shoulders when I heard the first screams.

I stilled for a moment before turning to peer out of one of the destroyed windows.

Dozens of vampires had emerged from the forest and descended onto the scattered passengers like a swarm of ravenous beasts. With a chill, I was reminded of the vampires on the *Demeter* as they began to tear into the flesh of the passengers with brutal and lethal efficiency.

I forced myself to look away from the gruesome sight of the massacre, quaking with fear. I had to focus on not letting my panic overwhelm me, and slowly removed one of my kukri knives from my sleeve, turning to move back towards the front door of the carriage, the straps of the bags now tied around my shoulders. Once I stepped out of the train, I would have to sprint to the tree line.

I was halfway to the carriage door when I heard a ferocious snarl, and a female vampire leapt inside the carriage, her fangs exposed as she trained feral black eyes on me.

18

GABRIEL

Trembling, I met her monstrous eyes.
Think, do not panic.
I could try to climb out of one of the shattered windows, but I knew that she would move too quickly for me to escape. I would have to fight her off.

My breathing was frantic as I clutched my kukri, keeping my eyes locked with hers. Her eyes shifted down to my blade, and I thought I saw her lips curl slightly, an oddly human movement, as if she were amused. She lunged forward with astonishing speed, landing on top of me and pinning me down with enormous strength. Her eyes were ferocious and pitch black as she reared down towards my throat, her fangs sharp and glinting.

Recalling what I'd done on the *Demeter* in the same precarious position, I twisted out of her reach, swinging out with my kukri in a sharp arc, my blade lodging into the side of her neck. Dark red blood spurted from the wound, and as she stiffened with a pained hiss, I yanked the blade out and sank it into her heart. She stilled, her eyes going from black to a very human hazel, and as her eyes met mine she looked . . . human. In that brief moment, I saw a glimpse of the vulnerable young woman she must have once been, her eyes displaying both grief and relief before they went blank. I yanked the blade from her chest as her lifeless body slumped forward.

I scrambled out from beneath her, stumbling towards the carriage door. I dashed out of the carriage, my muscles protesting with agony as I sprinted towards the tree line opposite the train tracks.

I didn't dare look back, but the cries of the passengers behind me were of a different sort this time. They were sounds of hopelessness and despair, of horror at their gruesome deaths at the hands of these creatures, echoing the cries of the dying shipmates aboard the *Demeter*—sounds I would never forget. I forced myself to keep running, pushing the image of the dying female vampire from my mind, and trying to block out the sounds of the screams.

Once I arrived in the sprawling dark forest, I picked up my pace, my legs screaming in pain with every footfall, struggling to maintain focus on the jagged path through the forest ahead. I soon made out two familiar forms—Abe and Seward. Abe moved slowly and painfully as Seward shouldered much of his weight, helping him along.

Flooded with relief at the sight of them, I started to pick up my pace, when I felt multiple cold gazes on my skin. The sensation came from the dense cover of trees that surrounded me. Multiple vampires were tracking me.

I deliberately slowed my pace. I couldn't lead them to Abe and Seward. My eyes filled as I watched Abe and Seward continue to limp forward, unaware that I was only yards behind them. *Stay alive*, I pleaded. *Stay alive.*

I turned to veer towards a tangle of trees away from them, praying that the vampires would follow me, not Seward and Abe. The cold sensation indeed trailed me, and as I stumbled towards the edge of a small clearing, lightly dappled by moonlight, I halted.

Four vampires were gathered, crouched in animalistic stances, their lethal eyes trained on me. They looked different than the feral vampires from the *Demeter* and the creatures back at the train wreckage. They appeared more controlled and refined, dressed in fine clothing like the vampires who had appeared at the Langham. If it weren't for their preternatural white skin and oddly colored eyes ranging from pitch black to blood red, I would have mistaken them for humans. But there was no denying their monstrous nature now as they hissed and snarled at me, preparing to strike.

I stood completely still, my heart wildly pounding in my chest. I had been fortunate with the previous vampire. How could I fight off several of them?

One of the male vampires straightened from his crouch to his full height of nearly seven feet; his red eyes glittering with recognition as he studied me, and I felt rather than heard his whispered word.

"*Ghyslaine.*"

The same word the vampire had whispered to me on Westminster Bridge. I was rattled by this, but maintained my focus on the matter at hand. I knew I couldn't outrun them, so I would have to take my chances in a fight. I could only pray that the wolfsbane tucked into my bodice would deter them, if not turn them away altogether, though it seemed to have no effect on the female vampire on the train.

It took a Herculean effort to remain still as I faced off with them, bracing myself for their attack. *Be prepared; but never be the first to strike. The one who makes the first move loses his advantage,* Sofia had once told me.

They all moved at once, eerily coordinated and impossibly fast as they launched themselves towards me. I took a step back and swung out my kukri, making contact with the neck of the first vampire. I yanked my blade free as she crumbled to the ground with a pained hiss and sunk it into the heart of the second vampire, pulling it out as a third vampire grabbed me by the neck and hurled me to the ground. I again tried to swing my blade as I lay prone, but the two male vampires crouched at my sides, pinning my arms to the ground in an inhumanly strong grip. I screamed, more in anger than in fear, that fate would have me die this way, the same way Father died, in a remote forest at the hands of a vampire.

One of the vampires reared down to my throat, sinking his fangs into the flesh. It was a horrible sensation, the feel of my blood flowing into the monster's hungry mouth. I closed my eyes, willing the darkness to take me, for a quick death . . . but something strange happened.

The fangs abruptly withdrew from my throat and my arms were released. My eyes flew open, and the two vampires retreated from me. The one who drank from me clutched his blood-stained mouth as he looked at me in horror. He turned to the other vampire, speaking in a language I did not recognize.

"*Li shi'l necre.*"

And they both vanished from the clearing.

FOR SEVERAL MOMENTS I sat there, stunned, searching amongst the trees for any sign of the vampires. But they had inexplicably retreated and left me alive.

I looked down at the wolfsbane, still tucked securely into my bodice. Perhaps the scent had deterred them. But doubt niggled at my mind, and I suspected that was not the case.

I stumbled to my feet, my eyes falling upon the two vampires I'd stabbed, who still lay crumpled on the ground. Grabbing my kukri, I staked the first vampire in the chest to avoid his possible resurrection, before turning to scramble out of the clearing.

I retraced my steps until I found my original path, my mind ablaze with questions as I ran. *Ghyslaine*. What was Ghyslaine? Did it have something to do with why had they left me alive?

I set my questions aside, focusing on locating Abe and Seward. I saw no sign of them. I fervently prayed that they'd made it unscathed to one of the abandoned farmhouses.

The trees seemed to watch me as I ran, but I felt no sensation of cold, vampiric gazes on my skin. I picked up my pace despite the persistent soreness of my limbs, eager to leave the dark forest behind.

I emerged from the forest onto a moonlit plain, where several farmhouses were dispersed across the countryside. I paused, unsure of which one Abe and Seward had taken shelter in, and decided to approach the closest one.

The door was partially open, and splatters of blood stained the entrance. Palming my kukri, I stepped inside. The room I entered appeared to be a kitchen, with dusty wooden floors, a small table and two chairs, a fireplace, and cupboards. It looked and smelled as if it had been in disuse for some time, and I wondered with unease what had happened to make the inhabitants leave.

The sound of muffled male voices came from the cellar. Familiar voices. Abe and Seward.

I descended the stairs. Abe was seated on the floor, propped up against the wall, the shrapnel no longer in his side as Seward bandaged the wound with his torn jacket. Abe was no longer bleeding, and though his face was crumpled with pain, some color had returned to his skin.

They both turned when I entered, looking relieved and then alarmed as they took me in. I followed their eyes. I had been so dazed with shock from my encounter with the vampires that I did not realize that I was splattered with blood, and still bled from the vampire's bite at my throat.

"Bloody hell, Mina," Seward gasped. "What happened?"

"Later," I said, hurrying forward to kneel down next to Abe. Seward was moving too slowly in bandaging up Abe's wound. "Let me do this. Did you clean the wound?"

"Yes," Seward said defensively, but he got to his feet and stepped back to let me finish securing the bandage. "Abe directed me. It was irritating."

"I did attend medical school," Abe said weakly,

a trace of wry humor in his tone. "You would have killed me had I not directed you."

"You need water," I said, irritated by their light-hearted banter. Abe was still wounded. "We're going to need better bandages while your wound heals, and I'm not sure how much blood you've lost, or if you'll need a—"

"The shrapnel was a surface wound. I have lost some blood but not enough to require a transfusion."

"I'll get water," Seward said, turning to hurry up the stairs as I continued bandaging his wound. Abe reached out to gently touch my arm.

"I will heal, Mina. The wound was not as grave as it appeared."

I nodded, but kept my eyes lowered. My relief was greater than he could possibly know, and I couldn't deny that it was linked to long-dormant feelings that now stirred beneath the surface of my awareness with aching familiarity. I was suddenly very aware of my hands on his bare skin, and hastily finished bandaging his wound, turning away from his perceptive eyes.

Seward returned with a bucket of water from a water pump in the rear of the farmhouse, along with a large cup from upstairs. I dipped the cup in the bucket and pressed it to Abe's lips.

"Now that we have confirmed I am not on the edge of death, are you going to explain why you are covered in blood?" Abe asked, after he took a long sip.

I used torn pieces of Seward's jacket to clean and bandage my neck wound as I told them of my encounter with the female vampire on the train, the vampires who had surrounded me in the clearing, the whispered word 'Ghyslaine', and their inexplicable action of leaving me alive.

They were both silent, until Abe looked at me with a concerned frown.

"Robert did not want you to return to Transylvania. This is all too much to be mere coincidence."

"Well, I don't know how. Or why," I replied, though I had to grudgingly acknowledge the truth of his words. "I didn't even know vampires existed until Father was murdered. And even then I remained in denial. No," I gasped, as a sudden dark thought occurred to me. "What if Jonathan was taken because of me? What if—"

"Do not let conjecture turn into needless worry," Abe gently interrupted.

"We haven't asked the most important question," Seward said, after another brief stretch of silence. "Why would vampires target those train tracks?"

"Easy prey?" I asked.

"Why make such a scene? The authorities and newspapers will cover this. They've mostly carried out their attacks in ways that can be explained away," Seward mused aloud, in full inspector mode.

"Perhaps they want to call attention to themselves," I said, unnerved by the thought.

"Or they're done hiding in the shadows."

The voice came from behind us. I reached for my kukri as I got to my feet and whirled around.

Gabriel stood at the doorway to the cellar, his grey eyes shot with fatigue, his shirt splattered with the dark blood of vampires. How had he entered so silently?

"I didn't mean to startle you," he said shyly, taking a cautious step into the cellar. "I saved as many passengers as I could, but many were still killed," he continued, his voice trembling with regret.

"Who the devil are you?" Seward asked, his eyes narrowed with suspicion. "Why've you been following us?"

Gabriel didn't look surprised by the question, but he stiffened, his eyes shifting to the floor. He was silent for so long that I feared he wouldn't answer. When he looked back up again, his entire focus was on me.

"I–I've been following Mina. Since before the *Demeter*. Long before that, actually. Much longer."

I went completely still. I recalled the coldness on my skin at Highgate Cemetery, Tilbury Docks, Amsterdam, the train, and my absolute certainty that it was a vampire's gaze.

I studied Gabriel even closer now. The preternatural flawlessness of his dusky skin and steel grey eyes. His great height. The jagged gash on his cheek from the derailment, which had already begun to heal.

Memories flashed through my mind. Gabriel had somehow survived the massacre aboard the *Demeter* and tonight's train derailment. He had warned me to get off the train before it derailed, as if he knew what was going to happen. And he had sensed the vampires' approach before they were even upon us.

A terrible dawning awareness burned my insides like the scorching flames of a fire. A realization that slammed into me with such force that I stumbled backwards, my hand flying to my mouth to stifle a cry.

Oh God, I thought, my turbulent emotions careening from astonishment to horror to panic to fury. How had I not seen this before?

He was one of them. He was vampire.

I was across the cellar in an instant, shoving Gabriel back against the wall, the blade of my kukri tight against his throat, my eyes wild with rage and tears.

19

REVELATIONS

From somewhere far away, I heard Abe and Seward cry my name. But my entire focus was centered on the man who stood before me. The vampire who stood before me.

"Monster!" I hissed, my blade pressed into his throat, drawing a thin trickle of dark red blood. Images flickered before my eyes, graphic and unbidden. The vampire hovering over Father's still form. The vampire standing before Jonathan at the Langham. Arthur dying on the small boat in the North Sea. The terrified final screams of the passengers at the site of the derailed train.

Gabriel evenly met my eyes, not flinching at the force of my rage or the pressure of my blade in his skin. In his eyes, I saw self-loathing, pain, and . . . surrender.

I felt Seward's firm hands on my shoulders, trying to push me back, but I shook him off. Gabriel did nothing to defend himself as he sank to his knees before me. I kept the blade against his throat as he moved. I wanted to kill him. I needed to kill him. For all that his kind had killed and destroyed.

"Mina," Abe whispered softly into my ear. He was behind me, but I didn't turn or back away from Gabriel. Abe's hand drifted down to mine, preventing me from pushing my blade further into Gabriel's skin. "He has saved our lives—and countless others—twice now. I do not believe he means us harm. Please, lower your blade. We need to hear what he has to say."

"He's vampire," I whispered rawly, unwilling to allow the reason of Abe's words to permeate my haze of fury. "He doesn't deny it."

"No," Gabriel said, his eyes steady on mine. "I don't deny it. I'm a monster."

"Silence," Abe said. "Do you want her to kill you? Why are you following her?" Abe continued, his hand steadfast on mine, and I could tell that with his injury he was using all of his strength to hold my blade still. "Who are you?"

"I made a promise to keep her safe," Gabriel said. Though he was addressing Abe, his eyes never left mine. "I gave her my word."

At his words, uncertainty flared, making me loosen my grip on the kukri. Abe moved quickly, yanking it from my hands and out of my reach. But I remained focused on Gabriel.

"Her? Who did you promise?" I demanded.

Gabriel's eyes were unwavering in their sincerity.

"Your mother, Mina," he said, and I heard the subtle tenderness in his tone at the word. "*Our* mother."

The room seemed to tilt on its axis; I took a halting step backwards, fervently shaking my head as both anger and confusion swirled through my mind.

"Liar!" I spat.

"We are blood, Mina," Gabriel continued. In the depths of his eyes I saw a small glimpse of longing, of hope. "I'm your only blood. I'm your half-brother."

I stared at him in a stunned daze, intensely aware of my heart thundering in my chest, the blood swirling through my veins, the deafening silence of the cellar.

He was lying. He had to be. I struggled to recall the faint memories I had of my mother. The loving smiles, the gentle embraces, the illness. Father's wan and worried face. *Your mother is not to be disturbed, Mina.* And then she was gone.

But there hadn't been another child. I would have remembered that. Even though I now knew Father kept secrets from me, I couldn't believe he would keep this to himself.

"You're lying," I repeated, but my words came out strangled and weak as I studied him. There was a nagging familiarity about him that I could not place. I took in his features, so unlike mine. But the eyes, though silver...

They were her eyes, I realized with horror. Gabriel's were a different color, but they were the same wide expressive eyes with the thick fringe of lashes that I recalled from both my memories and the photographs of her that I had gazed at longingly in the years after her death.

"You know I speak the truth," Gabriel said, as if reading my turbulent thoughts. He reached into his pocket, and I tensed, but he merely took out a locket, tossing it to the ground at my feet.

I reached down to pick it up. It was identical to the locket my mother had given me, a gold spinner locket engraved with her initials.

I opened it. Inside was a photograph of a young Gabriel—oddly beautiful, even as a child—seated on my mother's lap. It was similar to the photograph of me seated on her lap.

I pressed my hand to my mouth, tears springing to my eyes, as Gabriel continued to speak.

"She gave birth to me before she met and married your father. I don't know who my father was. I was raised by a kind human family in Thatcham, outside of London. She would visit me whenever she could. Before she died, she asked me to always look out for you as your older brother... and to make my presence known only when necessary."

I was still focused on the image of Gabriel and

my mother in the locket, trying to comprehend the enormity of what this meant, and it took several moments for his words to permeate. I looked up at him.

"Human family?" I asked unsteadily. "Why—why do you call them that? When were you turned into a vampire?"

"Turned?" Gabriel looked genuinely baffled, his brow furrowing into a frown. "I was never turned, Mina. I've always been vampire."

Another thunderous silence followed his words. I was still struggling with the realization that Gabriel—a vampire—was somehow my blood; this new information was almost too much to bear.

"You . . . you are saying—" Abe spoke up, shattering the strained silence, his voice quavering with horror and astonishment. "Your mother . . . *Mina's* mother . . . gave birth—"

"To a vampire. Yes," Gabriel said, and again I detected a self-loathing; a revulsion that was directed inward. "I asked her many times who my father was, but she refused to tell me anything about him. Mina, I know this is much to learn," he added, meeting my stricken eyes. "But Mother said I must only approach you when it was necessary. I– I was going to approach you years ago, when it seemed your father was close to discovering the existence of vampires. But when I learned the circumstances of his death, I knew you'd want nothing to do with my kind. I stayed away, but I kept watching you from a distance."

Beneath my shock, I felt a twinge of jealousy at his continual mention of my mother. He had known the mother I could barely remember. The mother who had kept his existence from me.

I closed my eyes, a gnawing frustration tearing at my stomach. When I'd left London, I thought my ignorance was only relegated to vampires. But now it included my own family.

"How do we know you're telling the truth?" Seward asked suspiciously.

"You don't. But I have no reason to lie." Gabriel's tone was firm with sincerity. "I–I wish I could have known life as a human. But I have always been this way. This . . . creature," he added, looking down at himself, his revulsion plain now.

"Did my father know of your existence?" I asked abruptly, both dreading and anticipating his answer.

"He knew Mother had another child prior to marrying him," Gabriel said, after a long moment of hesitation, and I saw concern in his eyes as he studied my taut features. "But he didn't know anything beyond that. He didn't know Mother still came to see me. He certainly didn't know that I'm vampire," Gabriel added quickly, as if trying to reassure me.

His words did nothing to quell the surge of

renewed hurt and anger I felt towards Father. This was yet another vital thing he'd kept from me.

"Are there others like you?" Abe asked. His horror had been replaced by his insatiable scientific curiosity, and I could practically see his mind churning. "How have you gone undetected for so long? What are your abilities?"

"Yes, there are many like me. We can remain undetected because we look human. I can see and hear exceptionally well, especially in the dark. And I can move quickly. Doctor Van Helsing, I will tell you more—much more," he said, as Abe opened his mouth to barrage him with more questions. "But you all must be exhausted. It's imperative that you sleep so that we can leave at first light. The authorities will soon arrive on the site of the train derailment. I assume you don't want to bring attention to yourselves by being questioned. We need to get Mina and you both back to England. These forests are not safe," he continued, addressing Abe and Seward.

"What do you mean, back to England?" I demanded, my astonishment shifting to anger. It pulled me from my shock, and I glared at Gabriel. "You're aware that I'm rescuing my fiancé from your murderous brethren. I will not return to England without him."

"I gave Mother my word that I'd keep you safe," Gabriel replied, his eyes hard with determination as he got to his feet, pulling himself to his intimidating height. "I thought I could keep you safe by shadowing you, but the vampires in these parts are ferocious. You all could have been killed tonight."

"We're aware of the danger," I returned. "I'm telling you that I will not return to England without Jonathan."

"I could easily overpower all three of you and force you back to England," Gabriel said, his tone turning dangerously soft, his silver eyes seeming to darken. I stiffened in spite of myself, but kept my eyes locked with his, not wanting to show him my trepidation. "But I'm giving you a choice," he continued, softening. "I know you're concerned about your fiancé. I can make inquiries, and see if I can—"

"Inquiries?" I snapped. "He was abducted by your kind. I will not abandon him. Even—even if you were to overpower us," I continued, hating how my voice quivered at the thought. "I will return. And keep returning."

Behind me, Abe and Seward kept quiet as Gabriel and I faced off. It was unnerving to stare into those familiar eyes, so much like my mother's, but I held my ground. Gabriel's existence was an earth-shattering revelation, but I would not be dissuaded from rescuing Jonathan.

"If you will not be persuaded to abandon this venture, then I am coming with you," Gabriel said.

Abe, Seward and I responded all at once.

"No." I snapped.

"That would be excellent." Abe said.

"Can you protect us from other vampires?" Seward asked.

Annoyed, I turned to glare at Abe and Seward. Seward flushed guiltily, but Abe held my eyes.

"Please leave us, Gabriel. I want to discuss this with my friends."

"You don't have a choice. I will follow you whether you agree or not," Gabriel said calmly, but he moved out of the cellar, ascending the stairs as quietly as he had come down them.

Once he was gone, Abe took a step towards me, grunting painfully as he moved, and I was pierced by a stab of guilt. With all the emotional chaos of Gabriel's revelations, I'd nearly forgotten about Abe's injury.

"Sit down," I urged, helping him to the floor and propping him gently against the wall. Abe leaned back against the wall, clutching his side before meeting my eyes, resolute.

"You must look past your emotions, Mina. Gabriel is vampire. He can—" he began.

"Exactly!" I interrupted.

"He knows their weaknesses. He is strong. He can help us," Abe continued, unwavering.

"He's saved our lives twice now. Do you believe he's your brother?" Seward asked.

I thought of Gabriel's familiar eyes. The locket. The tender way he spoke of my mother. The absolute sincerity in his tone. Despite my hatred of his kind, I could admit that there was something different about him—something almost human. And he was half human, impossible as it seemed.

"Yes," I grudgingly replied. "He has my mother's eyes. I know those eyes well. And I–I don't think he's lying. I don't know how it's possible, but he's of my blood."

"Then I'm with Abe. We need as much help as possible."

Gabriel had saved our lives twice now. He could help us. But I was still hesitant. Though my instincts told me that Gabriel wouldn't harm us, he was still part vampire. How could I ever bring myself to truly trust such a creature?

"You still have the wolfsbane, yes?" Gabriel's soft inquiry came from behind us, and we all turned. He had once again slipped noiselessly back into the cellar. I scowled at him.

"How do you manage to come and go so unobtrusively? Is that how you were able to follow us?" Abe asked, fascinated, studying Gabriel as if he were a new life form he had discovered in his laboratory.

"We asked for time alone," I said crossly, before Gabriel could respond.

"I can hear every word upstairs. I told you I hear exceptionally well. There was no point in my absence," Gabriel replied. "I have trained myself to move quite carefully, Doctor Van Helsing. Do you have the wolfsbane?" he repeated to me. "And your other weapons?"

"Yes," I replied, after a moment of hesitation. "Why?"

"Arm yourselves. Always have your weapons on hand. If that is what's necessary to make you feel safe around me, then very well," he said, betraying no emotion as he met our eyes.

"I do not think that—" Abe began.

"All right," I interjected. "If at any time we feel threatened by you—"

"You can stake me," he said, his face stoic as granite. "Moments ago, you almost did. I could have easily escaped—or harmed you—but I didn't. I think I have proven that I mean you no harm. I only want to honor Mother's wishes and keep you safe."

Abe and Seward nodded, looking thoroughly convinced. Gabriel gave me an inquiring look. I finally gave him a hasty nod of agreement. I would have to put my anxiety about him aside if I wanted to rescue Jonathan.

"There is a nearby town—Andorf—where we can collect horses and ride to the train station in Wels . . . it will take us in the direction of Transylvania," Gabriel said.

"How'd you know where we were going?" Seward asked, sounding more curious than suspicious now.

"I overheard you on the train." Gabriel replied.

"You were not seated anywhere near us," Abe

breathed, even more fascinated. "You will have to tell me more about your hearing."

"In time," Gabriel said, and despite the tense circumstances, I detected a slight trace of humor in his tone at Abe's transparent fascination with him. "I do want to suggest that we stop in Budapest for help before continuing on to Klausenburgh. I have friends there who may be able to help you."

"Friends?" I echoed, with an uneasy chill.

"Vampires," Gabriel said, once again reading my mind. "Before you protest, who are you looking for? The creature who took Jonathan, correct?"

"Of course," I said shortly.

"But you don't know who that is."

"We—we'll find out exactly who he is as we—" I hedged.

"My friends have lived in this region for some time. They may very well know the creature you're looking for, and perhaps even offer their assistance."

I looked at him, shaken. I barely trusted Gabriel, who was my blood and had saved our lives. But other vampires? I thought of the vampires I had encountered earlier in the clearing, with their bared fangs and black eyes. I shivered.

"We're not all monsters," Gabriel said. "I loathe creatures who attack innocents," he added, his eyes growing cold with hatred. "As do my friends. I trust them with my life. They have no interest in harming humans . . . they only wish to live in peace. The hour is late. Take the night to consider. But if you want to find and destroy the monster who took your fiancé, it will only be to your benefit to speak with them. They may have the answers you need."

There were an increasing number of questions that I needed answers to, but the thought of conversing with a group of vampires, or getting assistance from them, made me feel ill.

"Sleep. I think it's best for you all to remain in the cellar lest there are any more prowling vampires," Gabriel said, turning to move towards the cellar door. "I'll be outside."

He left us alone, and Seward and I gathered blankets from upstairs and prepared makeshift beds for Abe and ourselves in the cellar. I took the time to change out of my stained dress and into a clean one in an empty bedroom upstairs.

"You both realize that we must meet these other vampires," Abe said, when I returned, his eyes drooping with fatigue as he made himself comfortable on the blankets. "We do need answers."

"We'll discuss this tomorrow," I said. "Please get some rest. Call out if you are in any pain, or if you need anything at all."

Despite my fatigue, it took me a long while to drift to sleep as multiple questions raced through my mind about Gabriel. How had my mother come to give birth to a vampire? Why didn't she tell me or my Father of his existence? Would things have been different had I known?

When I finally slept, my dreams were filled with dark images of my mother, smiling lovingly at me until her lips curled back to reveal the sharp fangs of a vampire.

20

THE SILENT WAR

We awoke just after dawn the next morning, and Gabriel soon entered the cellar, politely informing us that he'd already brought over horses from Andorf, and they were waiting for us in the stables. Still reeling from the previous night's revelations, I was unable to meet Gabriel's eyes as I nodded my thanks.

"You traveled to Andorf and back quite expeditiously," Abe said, impressed, as he sat up.

I was relieve to see that Abe looked much better than he had the night before, though he was still slightly pale. His eagerness over having a real life vampire test subject seemed to outweigh any thought of his injury, and I practically had to order him to let me inspect his wound.

"I'm not as fast as full-fledged vampires, but I can move more quickly than humans. Andorf is not far from here, Doctor Van Helsing," Gabriel replied modestly, as I cleaned Abe's wound and applied the fresh bandages Gabriel had brought back from town.

"You have helped save my life twice. I insist that you call me by my Christian name," Abe said, giving Gabriel a kind smile, which he shyly returned.

I finished applying the bandages, slightly irritated at how quickly Abe had taken to Gabriel. We had decided that we'd take his advice and stop in Budapest for more information from Gabriel's friends, but I felt that we still needed to be on our guard around him.

Once Abe's wound was tended to, we ate the fresh bread that Gabriel had also brought with him. Gabriel didn't eat with us and hovered in the doorway as we ate. I wondered with a chill when he had last feasted on blood. Had he recently drained some poor villager?

I made myself push the disturbing thought away. It was best if I kept my thoughts away from his diet.

We moved to the upstairs rooms to wash and change into fresh clothes. My aches from the derailment had now dulled to soreness, and I grimaced as I changed into a grey traveling dress.

Abe was still too weak to ride on his own, so he shared a horse with me, leaning heavily against me and wrapping his arms around my waist. I had to focus on riding and ignored the familiar warmth of his body against mine as we rode away from the farmhouse.

Abe's full concentration was on Gabriel, who rode directly at our side. Abe must have shared my silent musings about Gabriel's diet, as he immediately began to pepper him with questions about what he ate. Dreading Gabriel's response, I tightened my grip on the reins.

"I have never taken blood from a human," Gabriel replied, and I sensed a hint of pride in his tone. "I find the act as deplorable as I'm sure you do. I do eat food, but I don't need as much and I don't find it satiating, unfortunately. My adoptive father was a butcher. He would bring home animal blood for me to consume. By the time I was twelve, a vampire I only knew as Uncle Quincy began to visit me regularly. He trained me to hunt and feed on animals. He also taught me how to abstain from consuming blood for up to two weeks."

"Who were your adoptive parents? How did they know about the existence of your kind?" Abe asked, his curiosity seeming to grow with the more answers that Gabriel gave him.

"Percy and Winifred Harris. They told me they had always known about vampires, but they never explained how. I don't know why my mother chose them, but I know they weren't able to have children of their own. They treated me—and loved me—as if I were their own," Gabriel said, his voice briefly catching as grief flickered across his features. "They died several years ago. My parents—and my mother—left me a small inheritance. It's been enough for me to travel and live without the risk of detection. Whenever I'm in England, I stay in their home."

Abe and Seward continued to ask Gabriel about his travels and abilities, while I remained silent, though I had a multitude of my own questions. I wanted to know more about my mother and how often she had visited him, what he knew about others of his kind, how long he had watched me. While he answered Abe and Seward's questions, I could feel his curious gaze slide periodically towards me, possibly wondering why I was so silent.

I needed time to come to terms with the knowledge that I had a half-brother who was a vampire; that there was so much about my own family I knew nothing about. My ignorance now seemed to form a great abyss, and every time I bridged a small gap, it grew even greater still.

"We've a theory, though we hope we're wrong," Seward said, his words cutting into my bleak reverie. "That the many vampire attacks throughout Europe—including the one last night—are due to some sort of invasion."

"I'm afraid you may be correct," Gabriel replied. "From what I have learned from my friends in Budapest, there has been a civil war amongst vampires for generations. I used to hear my parents whispering about it at night. The silent war, they called it. When Mother visited, I would hear her talk with them about it," he added, casting a sideways glance at me.

"My mother?"

I spoke in spite of myself, stunned. While it was quite obvious that she knew about vampires, how much more did she know? Exactly how much had she been involved in their world?

"Yes. But she never spoke of it to me," Gabriel replied. I could see a subtle relief in his eyes that I had finally spoken. "I know that though our numbers are low, there are many vampires who want to rule over humans."

"The vampire who took Jonathan," I began, gripped by a renewed fear. "Is he one of these vampires? Their leader, perhaps?"

"I don't know," Gabriel said, regretful. "Had I known anything of him, I would have come forward sooner. You have my word."

He met my eyes, and once again I saw nothing but truthfulness in his eyes. There was something unnerving about his sincerity. I thought of the revulsion I had seen on his face the night before, the self-hatred he'd tried unsuccessfully to hide. He'd been raised by humans, born to a human mother. Was it possible that he despised his own kind?

We soon arrived at Wels, where we were able to send post. Abe sent a letter to Greta, while I sent Clara a brief letter informing her that I was safely en route to Budapest. I briefly wondered if she knew of Gabriel's existence. Though there were secrets she had kept from me as well, I quickly dismissed the thought. Clara constantly worried about my chosen solitude and lack of friends in London. She would have eagerly welcomed a brother, even one that was vampire. In spite of myself, my lips twitched at the thought. Clara could always find the best qualities in anyone, and I had no doubt she would take an instant liking to Gabriel.

But would she ever meet him? When I returned to London, what role would Gabriel play in my life? Could I handle having a vampire as a permanent part of it?

Gabriel's intense gaze settled on me, as if he were reading my thoughts, and I turned away from him as we left the post office. There was no point in thinking of such things now. I had to focus on rescuing Jonathan.

We made a brief stop at a telegraph office. Peter Hawkins had responded to my wire. He informed me that he'd pulled Jonathan aside to inform him there had been yet another break in at their office only a few hours prior to the ball. Nothing had been taken, but it appeared the thief was looking for something. He urged me to keep him posted about my search for Jonathan as he was quite worried about him.

Guilt pierced me as I thought of Jonathan's tension at the ball. He must have already been on edge when he spotted me with Abe. I shared the wire with Abe and Seward, who looked concerned and flummoxed.

"It is reasonable to assume that the robberies are related to why he was taken," Abe said. "Do you know what he was working on at the firm?"

"No," I replied, frustrated. Jonathan rarely discussed details of his work with me, though I always inquired. "I do know that he often acted as an estate agent."

"What would vampires want with estate transactions?" Seward asked, baffled.

His question went unanswered, but remained on my mind as we left our horses at stables in the center of town and took a cab to the train station. News of the derailment at the border had spread, as we heard whispers of a rash of wolf attacks and decapitated bodies amongst the wreckage. A shiver ran through me as I recalled the horrors of the night before. None of these people could possibly imagine what had really happened.

We purchased our tickets for the next train to Budapest and boarded, finding seats in the rear compartment. Gabriel remained standing, informing us that he wanted to search the train for vampires or anything out of the ordinary.

"You can detect them?" Abe asked, intrigued.

"Most of the time, yes," Gabriel cryptically replied, before turning to head back down the aisle.

Abe looked gravely disappointed as he left; he had already taken out his journal, clearly intending to question Gabriel further. I could not hold back an amused smile, and Seward looked entertained as well. There had always been something endearing about Abe's rabid scientific curiosity, no matter what the circumstance.

"I have been doing research on animals as substitutes for years," Abe whispered, annoyed by our amusement. "Now I have an actual vampire to question and observe. One who is not trying to kill me, I might add. It would be like having Jack the Ripper in your custody," he added, as an aside to Seward.

"Not the same thing," Seward said, his amused smirk turning to a scowl.

"If Gabriel weren't my blood, I'd be just as eager to question him," I said, giving Abe an understanding nod. "But I fear that I will never quite recover from my shock."

"It will take time for this to settle. I can only imagine how you must feel. But the fact that he was born vampire," Abe added quietly. "It–it is simply astounding, Mina. It has been my conjecture that vampires can only be transformed by another. The notion that a human woman can give birth to one is . . ." he trailed off, shaking his head in wonder. "Imagine what we can learn from him."

"I know. But if my mother gave birth to him . . ." I whispered, finally speaking aloud the dark thought that had been circling through my mind. "Is it . . . is it possible that—"

"I think Robert would have noticed if your mother was not human," Abe whispered in reply, silencing me before I could complete the thought. "Which means that Gabriel's father—"

"Yes, I know," I interrupted, taking a cautious look around at the other passengers who were settling into their seats. We would have to continue our discussion in private, and Abe seemed to understand as he fell silent.

The train soon pulled away from the station, and my thoughts turned back to Gabriel's unknown father. I had thus far been focused only on my mother and her role in his life, not giving much thought to his father, who had to be vampire. That could only mean that my mother, the quiet and unassuming woman I'd briefly known as a child, had loved—and been intimate—with one of those monstrous creatures.

I suppressed a wave of revulsion at the thought. I knew nothing of my mother's life prior to Father meeting her. He only told me that she had been long estranged from her family, who lived somewhere in the French countryside. From the scant stories Father told me of her, I had put together a carefully constructed image of her in my mind. A devoted wife and mother who enjoyed playing the piano, reading, and telling me stories. A woman who, had she lived, would have become a less severe version of Mary Harker, without all of the snobbery; perhaps devoting her time to charity and helping the poor. But now it seemed that picture was an illusion, and she was a complete stranger to me.

I now understood that there was much I did not know about my parents, with all of the secrets they had kept from me. It seemed there was no reliable memory I could cling to. At the realization, a sudden sense of isolation crept over me, and I felt like a sailor marooned at sea in a storm, with no sense of when he would next see land.

"London is the largest city in the world," Abe whispered suddenly, his words pulling me back to the present. He had been furiously scribbling in his journal, but now set down his pen, looking shaken. "Jonathan handles estate transactions. For whom?"

"Clients who want to provide housing for the poor," I replied, wondering what he was leading to.

"What if . . . what if whoever took Jonathan wants information about this housing? Perhaps he wants to use lodging houses as some sort of base for his newly created vampires. Having vampires under his control residing in London would be an expeditious way of spreading vampirism throughout the city's population."

"Christ," Seward whispered. "I hope you're wrong, Abe."

"But why him? He's certainly not the only solicitor in London who handles estate transactions," I said.

"There were two other solicitors taken. I suspect they were taken for a similar reason. It is just a conjecture. There could be another reason for his abduction," Abe replied, with a hint of defensiveness.

I fell silent, considering Abe's theory. It was a reasonable one, and unease crept through me as I considered a base of vampires in London, poised to feast upon the masses. I prayed that Gabriel's friends could help us determine exactly who this creature was.

As the train approached the station in Budapest, Gabriel finally came to sit with us. He'd spent much of his time roaming up and down the aisle of the train or seated in different carriages, and only joined us for short, sporadic moments. He seemed to be consistently restless; whenever he was still, a sort of despondency seemed to settle over his countenance, a persistent sadness that seemed to be rooted somewhere deep. I wondered what his life must have been like, growing up vampire amongst humans, having a mother who loved him but kept him secret, all the while having another family in London. I felt a surprising flicker of sympathy for Gabriel, even as I tried to remind myself what he was, and that I should still be on guard around him.

When the train pulled to a stop, Gabriel gestured for us to follow him, and we trailed out of the station to find two cabs.

Seward and Gabriel took one cab while Abe and I took another. Our cabs took us away from the train station and through the Pest side of the city, which was marked by meandering cobblestoned streets and ornate baroque architecture. I had never been to Budapest, and I took in my surroundings with quiet awe, wishing that I were visiting under different circumstances.

We soon left Pest behind to cross the Szechenyi Chain Bridge to the Buda side of the city on the opposite side of the Danube River, which glittered beneath the fading light of the setting sun. In Buda, we made our way down the old medieval streets of the Castle District, where we were dropped off at the edge of Vienna Gate Square, an area that teemed with both shops and old homes that were both baroque and medieval in appearance.

Gabriel seemed quite familiar with these streets, and we followed him as he walked brusquely towards a row of homes with yellow stucco and greystone facades on the far edge of the square. He approached a gated home, casually opening the unlocked gate, and led us across the front courtyard and into the front doors.

As we entered the long narrow entrance hall, I

hesitated, wondering where the other vampires were. But Gabriel continued down the hall without pause. Abe and Seward trailed behind him. I reluctantly followed as Gabriel led us to a grandiose drawing room.

It was the largest drawing room I had ever seen. The wooden floors were covered by oriental rugs; the walls dominated with paintings portraying idyllic scenes of nature. The plush couch and chairs were made of fine brocade and silk, which gleamed in the sunlight that filtered in to the room from the windows. I realized that this was far too grand to be an ordinary home. It looked as if it belonged to someone of the nobility.

"Whose home is this?" I asked Gabriel.

"Radu Draculesti. He's occupied this home for quite some time," Gabriel replied. "I came to Budapest years ago, after my parents died. Radu lets me stay here when I visit. He is one of the kindest creatures I know—vampire or human. He will help you. He knows we are coming, I sent him a wire. He will be here shortly."

I stiffened at the name Draculesti. Both Abe and Seward met my eyes across the room. The Draculesti had been one of the families who once occupied the fortress we were heading to in Transylvania. Could there somehow be a connection?

"What is it?" Gabriel asked. He hadn't missed our exchanged look.

"The name seems familiar," Abe vaguely

replied. "We will have to ask your friend some questions about it."

If Radu knew something, it could help us greatly. But what if Gabriel was wrong about him? What if Radu was connected to the fortress, and he was dangerous? Had we inadvertently walked into some sort of trap?

I studied Gabriel, who now stood quietly near the doorway, his silver eyes trained on me. There was no hint of deception in their depths, no malice.

I willingly calmed myself, moving over to study one of the paintings on the wall; it was one of the few that didn't depict a scene from nature. In the painting sat a lovely woman with long dark hair and bright green eyes. She wore an elaborate eighteenth century dress of deep red silk with a large hoop skirt. She sat posed on a settee in what appeared to be this very room, her expression serene but sad. As I studied it, wondering who she was, I felt ice on my skin, and turned to face the doorway.

Two vampires hovered there. A beautiful female vampire of Asian descent, with long raven black hair, dark eyes, high cheekbones and a generous mouth, stood next to a tall male vampire who looked vaguely familiar, with a pointed angular face framed by dark hair, his skin so white it was nearly translucent. The female vampire's eyes seemed to darken with hostility when they landed on me, and as Gabriel stepped forward to address them, we were suddenly slammed back against the far wall by an invisible force.

Panicked, I realized that this was the same sensation I'd felt at the ball and on the *Demeter*. I was paralyzed, and my throat began to close as I struggled to breathe. The edges of my vision dimmed, and I began to slip from consciousness.

21

DRACULESTI

As darkness filled my vision, I dimly heard Gabriel's cries.

"Anara, release them! That is my sister! They are here for your help!"

"Release them!" the male vampire demanded, and we were immediately released from the paralyzing hold, collapsing to the floor like puppets without their strings.

My vision cleared, and I struggled to catch my breath. Gabriel hurried towards me, helping me up. I was still dizzy and I swayed slightly on my feet as his worried grey eyes locked on mine.

"I'm all right," I managed to rasp, turning to focus on Abe and Seward. Seward had gotten to his feet as well, his hands on his knees as he hunched forward, sucking in deep breaths of air. Abe remained huddled on the floor, looking deathly pale.

"Abe . . ." I whispered, kneeling down to his side.

"I just need to breathe," he said weakly, allowing me to help him to his feet.

"Why did you do that?!"

I turned. Gabriel was now advancing towards Anara, his eyes blazing with fury. Anara remained rigid, her hostile eyes still centered on us. At her side, the male vampire whom I assumed was Radu, also gave her a hard look.

"I brought them here for your help, and you nearly kill them!" Gabriel continued, furious. "They already fear our kind. Last night they were nearly killed by a pack of ferals."

I saw a flicker of what may have been guilt dart across Anara's features, but it was quickly masked. Radu stiffened at Gabriel's words.

"Ferals?" he asked sharply, his English accented with both Romanian and another language that I could not identify. "How many?"

"Around fifty. Perhaps more," Gabriel replied. Though he spoke to Radu, he still glared at Anara. "I saved as many humans as I could, including my sister and her friends. Anara could have—"

"Your sister's hatred dripped off her like poison," Anara snapped, tearing her eyes away from us to focus on Gabriel. Her voice was surprisingly soft for a creature who emanated such hatred. "She's armed with a kukri. That blade is made to kill our kind! Are they all armed?"

"It was the only way they would feel safe traveling with a vampire," Gabriel returned. "Now I understand why. You're stronger than all three of them combined! They mean you no harm."

"All humans mean us harm!" she cried. Beneath the fury of her words, I sensed a raw vulnerability. "You will never understand—you are one of them!"

"This bickering serves no purpose," Radu said, holding up his hand to prevent Gabriel from responding and turning to face us. Unlike Anara, I only saw kindness in his eyes. "I must offer my sincerest apologies to all of you. I never should have allowed my daughter to put you into a thrall, but I am afraid that she distrusts humans."

I frowned, looking at Anara, whose face remained stormy. How could Anara be his daughter? They were of different races, and he looked no more than ten years older than her.

He stepped towards us, and I nearly gasped at the true breadth of his height. He appeared to be nearly seven feet tall, towering over all the men in the room. I forced myself to not shrink back as he continued forward, extending a long, tapered hand towards us in a gesture of greeting.

"I am Radu," he said, his politeness shaded with warmth. "Gabriel has told me of you, Wilhelmina." It was odd to be called my full name. Clara and Father rarely used it, but it fell naturally from Radu's lips. "It is my assumption that this gentleman is your fiancé?" he inquired, his eyes sliding towards Abe.

"He's not my fiancé," I interjected, flushing. "This is Doctor Abraham Van Helsing, and this is Inspector Jack Seward of Scotland Yard in London."

"It is my deepest pleasure to meet you all," Radu said, with an amiable nod. "You have been acquainted with my daughter Anara," he continued, gesturing towards her with a surprising trace of humor. "Again, I must apologize for her actions. May I offer you tea or food? You must be famished after your journey."

I was taken aback by his kindness. Though I sensed the same genuine sincerity from him that Gabriel displayed, I remained hesitant. How could Radu be so kind and Anara so hostile? My eyes strayed nervously towards Anara, who still glared openly at us. Radu followed my gaze.

"I will not allow Anara to harm you. If it puts you at ease, she will not remain in the room with us."

"Radu—" Anara protested.

"Silence, my love," he said, the endearment contradicting the harsh look he directed towards her. "You have frightened Gabriel's sister and her friends. Please leave us while I speak with our guests."

Anara's eyes flashed with anger, but she obligingly left the room. Radu gestured for us to sit at the small round table in the center of the room before disappearing briefly and returning with a tray of tea. I was surprised. From the quiet grandeur of his home, I would have expected a small army of servants.

"I am unable to keep servants for long. My daughter frightens them," Radu said, by way of explanation, giving us a rueful smile as he set down the tray, and I was again struck by his amiability. Radu was a large and intimidating vampire, yet I felt increasingly comfortable in his presence. He folded his lengthy body into the chair across from us. "What is the matter you require my assistance with?"

"My fiancé Jonathan was abducted from London by a group of vampires," I replied. "We're traveling to a fortress in Transylvania where we believe he's being held, but we don't know who took him."

Radu stilled before handing us each a cup of tea, his piercing black gaze settling on me. I was coming to learn that vampires had a disconcerting manner of not breaking eye contact, and I shifted in my seat at his scrutiny.

"Where is this fortress located?" he asked.

"A vampire under hypnosis told us it's located in the Carpathians, in some sort of 'old home'," I replied, recalling Lucy's words. Abe reached into his bag and handed Radu his crumpled map of the region.

"We recognized your last name," Abe said, as Radu studied the map. "Our research indicates that the Draculesti were one of the families to occupy this fortress at some point in the past. Is that correct?"

Radu grew even more pale as he stared down at the map. I didn't know if he was reacting to Abe's words or to the map itself.

"Yes," Radu said. When he looked up, I saw a faint shimmer of blood red tears, and I had to will myself not to recoil in shock and revulsion at the sight. "And I believe I know who presently dwells there."

All of the air seemed to suck out of the room. Abe, Seward and Gabriel all froze. In Radu's eyes, I now saw a maelstrom of pain, regret—and guilt.

"They are the last descendants of one of the oldest vampire families in Europe. They long to restore their family name to its previous glory. They are my children," he whispered. "It is my family. I am the monster you seek."

IN THE STUNNED space of silence that followed Radu's words, I stumbled to my feet, my hand instinctively reaching for the kukri that was tucked in my sleeve, while Abe, Seward and Gabriel remained frozen with shock. Anara must have somehow sensed the tension in the room, because she was instantly back in the drawing room and at Radu's side in a flash of movement, crouched in a protective stance, her eyes blazing in my direction.

"I will tear out your throat if you attempt to harm him!" she hissed.

I didn't move, barely heeding her presence. I was still reeling from Radu's words. He was the monster we sought? Was he working with the vampires who had taken Jonathan—his children? Had Gabriel brought us into some sort of trap after all? I looked at Gabriel, but he looked just as stupefied as I felt.

"I am responsible for all of this," Radu continued, his voice dropping with sorrow. "I deserve your wrath."

"Radu, silence!" Anara shouted, before turning to her focus back to me. "Lower the kukri. I will kill you!"

"You'll not harm my sister, Anara," Gabriel managed to bite out in warning, though he still looked shaken.

"What do you mean? Explain!" I demanded from Radu, ignoring Anara and maintaining a solid grip on my kukri.

In a quick blur of movement, Anara sprang towards me and yanked the kukri from my hand before retreating back to Radu's side. I blinked, astonished by the rapid movement. Abe, Seward and Gabriel instantly rose to their feet, crowding protectively around me.

"Please. Answer me," I pleaded, my voice quavering as I returned my focus back to Radu. "What are you—"

"Radu's biological children have been carrying out the attacks and abductions around Europe. Vlad and Ilona," Anara said, spitting out the names like they were a bitter poison. "They are evil. Father," Anara said, her voice softening as she rested her hand on his shoulder. "Their evil is no fault of your own."

Vlad and Ilona, I thought with a daze. I recalled the male and female vampire at the Langham. Were they the children of the anguished vampire who sat before me? *Two as one*, Lucy had said. Brother and sister . . . working together? Two leaders?

Dazed, I sank back down into my chair, as Abe, Seward and Gabriel followed suit. I leaned forward, pressing my forehead against my trembling fingertips, and I forced myself to speak.

"Where . . . where are they now?" I asked.

"I do not know, I swear it," Radu answered swiftly. "If I did, they would not be causing so much destruction. I would do what needs to be done. They must be stopped. I understand that now."

"Now?" Seward asked, his eyes narrowed. "Did you have the chance to stop them before?"

"Do not speak harshly to him," Anara snapped. "You do not know what—"

"Anara, it is all right. They have a right to know everything. Especially Wilhelmina," Radu said quietly, his regretful eyes holding mine. "Yes, I did have the chance to kill them once, but I could not do it. How could I? They are my blood. My son calls himself Vlad, after the many voivode rulers from our line. But my beloved—my now departed wife Ludmila—" He paused, his gaze straying to the painting on the wall of the sad, green-eyed woman. "She named him Alexandru. Alexandru and my daughter Ilona shared the same womb. We soon realized they share the same evil nature. Alexandru became particularly obsessed with the past great rulers of our line—their cruelty, their power. As he grew older, I realized that he wanted to restore our line to its previous glory. Ilona was not as desperate for power as my son. He has been the true leader, and she his most loyal follower; she loves him so."

Radu stopped speaking for a moment, a bloody tear trickling down his cheek.

"I tried to make my son understand the reason our line died out was because of our obsession with power. Centuries of infighting cannibalized our ancestors. But I could not reach him—nor could my Ludmila. I knew there was no hope when my children massacred a small human village for sport when they were barely adults. Ludmila was so heartbroken at the monsters that they had become, she starved herself to death. But even this did not affect my children," he continued, his voice dropping to a raw whisper. "Vlad began to gather followers—human and vampire alike. Vlad wanted to rule over not just the humans—but other vampires as well. He destroyed all who opposed him. As he gained more power, he gained more followers. Many of our kind fought against him."

"Vlad was the cause of the civil war?" Gabriel asked, horrified.

"One of the causes, yes. He was not the only vampire who wanted power, but they came the closest to an all-out invasion. With the disappearances and massacres, they were bringing potential attention to vampires, which risked our annihilation. Humans still greatly outnumber us; it is why we live in the shadows. That is when it was decided that—that they needed to be executed," he added, with great difficulty. "But I . . . I could not bear—"

Radu's voice caught, and Anara kneeled down at his side. Her eyes shimmered with tears of blood as well. She took his hands, pressing her lips to his knuckles.

"*Este de inteles, tata,*" she whispered.

Her words seemed to give him the strength to continue, and he turned back to face me.

"Several members of the Order—I do not know who, I could not bear to know—tracked my son to a forest in central Transylvania, where he was preparing to carry out more attacks on human villages. There was a violent confrontation—many died—but the attempt to kill him failed. He was left on the verge of death, and it is believed that he survived in a weakened state for years somewhere in Transylvania. He must have subsisted off of animals, the occasional human—whatever it took to keep his strength for all those years. My daughter was not with him, and no one was able to track her down. The attacks on humans ceased, and I thought their threat had been eliminated. Three years ago, rumors began to spread about his resurrection and the regrouping of his followers. The attacks on humans began once more."

"How many followers do your children have?" Abe asked. "How many oppose them?"

"I do not know their numbers, but there are many. We believe that the feral packs of vampires, like the ones you came across, are of their creation. Newborn vampires not given time to adjust to their hunger or abilities. They move quickly and kill many. As for those who oppose them—they are not as many as his followers, I am afraid. Many have gone into hiding for fear of retribution."

My thoughts raced in a frantic blur. Three years ago. The forest in central Transylvania. That was where I had witnessed the creature feasting on my father. I recalled its torn and ragged flesh, its cold eyes on me—the same eyes I felt at the Langham and on the Westminster Bridge.

My entire body went cold as the revelation slammed into me with the force of a sledgehammer.

The creature who had taken Jonathan and killed my father were one and the same—Radu's son. And now I had a name. Vlad Alexandru Draculesti.

I repeated the name in my mind, over and over again, until it was a litany, and I felt a swell of rage so great that my entire body began to shake.

"My . . . my father—" I whispered. "He was killed in the forests of Transylvania three years ago by a weakened vampire. Abe and I saw it happen."

The silence stretched as Radu met my stare, his eyes widening in horror.

"Oh, Wilhelmina," he breathed. "I heard Vlad killed a human to fully restore himself. I did not know. I am . . . I am so sorry."

I lurched weakly to my feet. Abe buried his face in his hands, while Gabriel and Seward studied me with sympathy and concern. Anara moved protectively closer to Radu, as if preparing for me to strike. But my rage had already begun to subside, transforming back to the grief that had been my constant companion since Father's death.

"I–I need—" I began. I felt claustrophobic and struggled to breathe, as I had in the Langham a few nights ago when Abe had whispered in my ear that the creature from Transylvania was in London, and I uttered the same words. "I need air."

Not waiting for a response, I turned and stumbled from the room. I made my way out of the drawing room, out the front door and into the courtyard, sinking to my knees as I took in great gasps of air.

The sheer enormity of all I had learned sank down onto my shoulders like a great weight. Legions of vampires living in our midst. A secret war between them. A half-brother who was vampire. Parents who kept a multitude of secrets from me. Confirmation that Father had died at the hands of this Vlad. And Jonathan, innocent and unaware of any of this, imprisoned at the hands of monsters who wanted to take over the human world.

I closed my eyes, once again longing for my previous ignorance; my peaceful life back in London with Jonathan, Clara and my students, and no knowledge of this hidden world that was possibly about to bring mine to an end.

Footsteps approaching from behind me brought me back to the present, and I climbed back to my feet. Abe and Seward approached me cautiously, as if I were a wounded animal.

"I'm quite all right," I said. "There was no need for you to—"

"You are not all right," Abe interjected.

He stepped forward to enfold me in the comforting warmth of his arms, and I allowed the tears that I had been holding at bay to fall, thinking of not only my father and Jonathan, but of all the victims of these monsters, and the immensity of the fight that still lay ahead.

When my tears subsided, I stepped out of Abe's arms, and we all stood in somber silence.

"We know who took Jonathan. Radu can find and kill his son," Seward said. "We can return to London, and let them fight their own—"

"No," I said swiftly. "I won't turn back now, Seward. I'm too close to rescuing Jonathan."

"Mina, you heard him. Vlad has many followers," Seward said, frowning. "We don't have the—"

"I'm not returning to London without Jonathan!" I cried, staring at him in disbelief. "And now that I know my father died at Vlad's hands, I won't let my fiancé suffer the same fate."

"What if he already has?" Seward asked bluntly.

"Jack!" Abe cried.

"Then I will avenge him," I returned, though the thought of Jonathan's possible death sent a spiral of grief through the pit of my stomach. "As I will avenge my father, and Arthur, and Lucy, and all the deaths that monster is responsible for!"

I was now keenly aware that this journey was about more than rescuing my fiancé. It was about stopping the impending threat of vampires from taking over the human world. I had severely underestimated the treacherous path that lay ahead of us when we'd left London. The best weapons and a small army of vengeful villagers wouldn't be enough to take on Vlad, Ilona and his followers. I knew what we had to do going forward, though a rush of dread filled me at the thought.

"Radu said that there are other vampires who oppose Vlad. We need to ally ourselves with them to destroy him," I said, meeting their eyes. "We need to join the war."

Read FORTRESS OF BLOOD (Mina Murray Book 2) or the <u>complete series omnibus</u> now.

THE MINA MURRAY SERIES OMNIBUS

 **This omnibus also includes <u>Shadows of Night</u>, a bonus collection of prequel short stories.*

<u>Praise for the Mina Murray Series</u>

"...I was blown away by how much I enjoyed *The Beast of London*. The characters, setting and plot were all phenomenal..."—Dual Reads

"...*The Beast of London* is an exceptional book with compelling characters, an intricate plot and plenty of "I didn't see that coming" moments." —Knockin Books Reviews

"I love a good Dracula retelling and ... *The Beast of London* is action-packed and filled with danger and adventure." —With Love for Horror Books

FORTRESS OF BLOOD PREVIEW

Soon after our meal, Szabina gathered all the humans who were to fight in the central courtyard, ordering us to bring our weapons with us. Anara, Radu, Gabriel, and several other vampires moved to stand in an intimidating row in front of us.

Despite her petite stature, I could tell that Szabina commanded much respect; she held everyone's attention as she stepped forward, her multicolored eyes continually straying towards me as she addressed us in Romanian, and then English.

"We are strong and we are fast. Many of us can hold our prey in thrall," Szabina said, her voice carrying across the courtyard. "But we do have weaknesses. We can be staked or beheaded. Aim for here, or here," she said, pointing to her heart, and then her throat. "Anywhere else may wound us, but not kill. For the thrall, avoid looking in the eyes . . . that is how we enter your mind."

She stopped speaking for a moment, allowing her words to settle. Next to me, Seward and Abe listened intently, and I could practically see Abe sorting the information in his mind to be added to his journal later.

"Make certain you have your weapons. None of us will harm you, but the vampires at Vlad's fortress will try to rip you apart," she concluded darkly.

I held one of my kukri knives in my left hand; the second one and a knife were securely stowed in my sleeves and the bodice of my dress. Around me, the other humans clutched knives and makeshift wooden stakes. Abe and Seward stood at my side. Seward had lost his revolver in the train derailment, and was now armed with two of Abe's knives.

Szabina nodded to the other vampires, and they moved into predatory crouches. Though I knew they would not harm us, apprehension filled me at the sight. Even Radu and Gabriel, whom I had slowly come to trust, looked lethal in their crouched positions.

Szabina did not give us the order to run; she and the other vampires merely sprang towards us at an impossibly fast speed.

My instincts set in, and I turned on my heel to race towards the open gates and out of the village, dashing into the depths of the surrounding forest with the other humans.

Seward, Abe, and I kept pace together as we

ran, but a vampire soon tackled Seward to the ground from behind, while another grabbed Abe and slammed him against a tree.

I halted when the vampire grabbed Abe, raising my kukri to intervene, but Abe's eyes met mine as he struggled with the vampire.

"Run, Mina!" he shouted.

I had to remind myself that this was a training exercise; they would not harm Abe. But I was still fearful as I raced away from him.

I only made it a few yards when a hand gripped my neck and pinned me down to the ground from behind. But the grip was gentle, and I twisted around to see Gabriel hovering above me.

"You need to fight me, Mina," he said. "You can wound me. I will heal."

I tried to yank myself out of his grip, but he was far too strong. I turned back to look at him, hesitant. My growing trust made me reluctant to wound him; I could not believe that I'd nearly killed him only two days ago.

Seeing my continued hesitation, Gabriel yanked my head backward, more roughly this time, and bared his teeth. At the sight, my instincts took over, and I swiftly sank my kukri back into his shoulder. Gabriel let out a howl of pain, loosening his grip, and I stumbled to my feet to scramble away.

The trees whipped past me as I ran, and through the forest depths I could vaguely hear frantic shouts and cries as the other humans fought off the vampires. But the sounds became more distant as I ran, and I soon found myself in a dark patch of forest.

The trees grew closer together here, their density allowing very little sunlight to filter through their coiled branches—a dark prison erected by nature. A sense of dread crept over me, and I turned to race back towards the village.

But as soon as I turned, I heard a vicious snarl from the black depths of the forest behind me, and felt the cold gaze of a vampire. Had I stumbled across a random feral roaming through the countryside? Had I strayed too far from the others?

I started to dash out of the clearing, lifting up my skirt to pick up my speed, but when I heard the swift cracking of twigs and snapping of branches behind me, I knew the vampire was racing towards me and would soon overtake me. I continued to run, opening my mouth to let out a desperate scream to alert the others.

A cold hand reached out and gripped me by my neck from behind, as Gabriel had done only moments earlier, abruptly cutting off my scream. This time, the hold was far rougher than my brother's grip had been.

My captor yanked me around. It was Anara, but I felt no relief at the sight of her; her eyes were ferocious and filled with the promise of violence.

She dropped her hand from my throat. Her

gaze remained trained on mine as my body lifted from the ground, and I was slammed hard against a nearby tree. Unable to move, terror flooded me as Anara stalked towards me like a wolf approaching fresh prey. When she reached me, her hand again went to my throat, her eyes burning like fire. Her hand tightened around my throat and I panicked as I struggled to breathe.

We were completely alone in the clearing, and her face showed no hint of mercy as she continued to squeeze the air from my lungs. I had no way to defend myself, no way to fight back.

I did not know why Anara hated me so, but even with her hand on my throat, I knew instinctively that she wasn't evil. There was more to her, a pain and humanity that was absent from the mindless ferals I had encountered. I raised my eyes to hers in desperation, pleading with my eyes for her to release me. But when my eyes locked with hers . . . something strange happened. I saw something. Felt something.

I was a young girl, my reed thin arms wrapped around my legs as I wept and rocked myself back and forth, seated in the center of the splintered wooden floor of a tiny cottage that had been ransacked; furniture and scraps of food were scattered about. In front of me, a man and a woman—my parents?—were being dragged away by a group of men.

"Please! Don't harm my little girl!" the woman

screamed. Her pain was palpable; her body wracked with grief and terror. "Leave my Anara be! Please, she has done nothing! I beg you!"

"Take me, please!" the man begged. "Leave my wife and child alone. Kill me, not them! Please!"

"Mama!" I screamed. The word was thin and my throat was strained, as if I had been crying for days. I scrambled to my feet and raced towards my parents. "Papa!"

One of the men stepped forward and backhanded me, sending me sailing across the room, and I hit the wall with such force that I slipped from consciousness.

And then the scene was gone. I was back in the present, crouched on my hands and knees on the ground, coughing and gasping for breath. Anara had stumbled away from me, her hands pressed to the sides of her head, looking dazed.

I was disoriented by what I had seen, but my self-preservation kept me focused, and I reached for the kukri that had dropped to the ground, holding it out defensively should she try to attack me again.

But Anara made no move towards me, her eyes clouded with confusion as she looked at me, her breathing ragged. We stood at a stalemate for several moments, until I dimly heard multiple footfalls approach the clearing.

"Mina!" Abe shouted as he raced into the clearing, his eyes sweeping over me with fretfulness. "I heard you scream. Are you—"

"I'm . . . I'm all right," I said hastily, as other humans and vampires began to file into the clearing.

Gabriel hurried into the clearing, pushing past the others, his gaze straying suspiciously from me to Anara. When he saw my throat, he grabbed Anara and pinned her to a tree, his lips curled back in a ferocious snarl.

"Did you harm my sister?" he roared.

But Anara was unfazed by Gabriel's fury. She was still focused on me, her confused expression shifting to one of suspicion.

"How did you do that?" she demanded, ignoring Gabriel. "You were in my mind. You did something to me!"

"You are far stronger and she's the one who is bruised! Answer me!" Gabriel shouted.

"What is happening?" Szabina asked sharply. She and Radu entered the clearing, moving past the cluster of humans and vampires who had gathered.

"She attacked my sister!" Gabriel snapped.

"Anara. I already warned you—" Radu began, looking furious.

"I–I wasn't going to kill her! She was able to release herself from the thrall, which is impossible!" Anara cried, pointing a quivering finger at me. "She was in my mind. I felt her!"

Szabina stiffened at her words, and I saw alarm flicker in her eyes.

"Harming the humans is forbidden," Szabina said, disregarding Anara's words, her voice strained.

"You are dismissed from the training," Radu added. "I will discuss this with you later. Please escort her back to the village," he quietly ordered two hovering vampires, who approached Anara.

"Listen to me! She looked at me, I felt something in my mind, and I could no longer hold her in thrall. No human has ever done that to me before!" Anara cried fervently, as the two vampires gripped her arms to lead her away.

But Radu and Szabina didn't look at her, and once she was gone, Szabina approached, studying me closely.

"Is that true?" she asked. "You released yourself from the thrall?"

A hush fell as Abe, and all the others who were gathered, turned curious and awestruck looks towards me. I flushed, suddenly feeling oddly defensive, as if I had done something wrong.

"I–I just looked into her eyes, and I saw—I think I saw something from Anara's childhood. It was like a dream. Or a memory. Her parents were being dragged away."

Radu went rigid at my words, frowning. The silence stretched.

"Perhaps it was my desperation," I said hastily, unable to bear the silence or the strange looks the others were giving me. "If one of you can put me into another thrall, I can show you all what I did, and then—"

"No," Gabriel interjected. "It is too dangerous, and there's no guarantee you will be able to release yourself again."

"We need to learn to defend ourselves against the thrall! It's one of your most powerful weapons," I protested. "If I can teach others to do what I just did, our chances against Vlad and his followers are even greater."

"I agree with Gabriel," Abe said, looking worried. "It is far too dangerous."

"My daughter was right," Radu spoke up, looking at me intently. "We are not aware of any other human who has been able to release themselves from the thrall. Others here may not be able to do the same."

Tendrils of unease curled around me as everyone continued to look at me like I was a newly discovered specimen. What did it mean that I was able to break the thrall? Yet another question to add to the mountain of unknowns.

"We are losing time. Let us take a break from the training," Szabina said. "We meet back in the courtyard."

Everyone began to scatter, casting curious glances at me as they did so. Abe, Seward, and Gabriel approached me, and beneath their polite urgings for me to get some rest, I could see the inquisitiveness in their eyes at this newly discovered ability of mine.

I barely listened to their words. My focus was on Szabina, who remained at the edge of the clearing, watching me with turbulent eyes, before she turned to head back towards the village.

"Are you listening?" Abe asked impatiently. "I want to examine your neck to see if there—"

"Wait here," I said shortly, leaving them behind as I hurried after Szabina. I was determined to find out the cause of her frequent looks.

She seemed to sense that I was following her, as she picked up her pace. Worried that she would use her vampiric speed to evade me, I quickly jogged forward to move in front of her, blocking her path.

"You keep looking at me. Why?" I demanded.

When Szabina stiffened, averting her eyes, I knew that my inkling was correct. She knew something, and for whatever reason, she was hiding it from me.

"Szabina, please. Do you know something about me?" I pressed. "There is so much that I don't know about my own past, my own life. If you know something, please . . ." my voice broke, and I had to blink back my tears.

Compassion flared in her eyes, and she expelled a long breath.

"I did not want to believe it at first . . . I still cannot," she said. "But I have only seen one human break the thrall of a vampire, and I have lived many years. Do you know the name Ghyslaine?"

I froze as my heart began to pummel against my ribcage. Ghyslaine. It did mean something—something vital. I could see it in her eyes. And she knew my connection to it.

I felt a sudden and strange sense of stillness; like the calm right before a violent storm. I had felt it right before Gabriel revealed his identity, and the night that I stumbled into that clearing to find my father's dead body. It was the sense that everything would soon change, and my world would not be the same.

Szabina's vivid eyes were now shimmering with blood tears. She stepped forward, placing cold trembling hands on the side of my face, gazing at me with a look of near reverence.

"Wilhelmina Murray," Szabina whispered. "I know who you are."

Read FORTRESS OF BLOOD (Mina Murray Book 2) or the complete series omnibus now.

ALSO BY LAUREN GOFFIGAN

The Mina Murray Series

The Beast of London

Fortress of Blood

Realm of Night

Mina Murray Complete Series Omnibus: Books 1-3

Greek Goddesses Collection

The Goddess

Medusa

Celtic Queens Collection

The Celtic Queen

The Iron Queen

ABOUT THE AUTHOR

Lauren Goffigan writes rich, character-driven historical fiction and historical fantasy. She enjoys exploring fierce and complex heroes and heroines of the past and bringing them to life in the present.

When not writing, you can find her traveling to places she's never been, reading the latest book which strikes her fancy, or watching a documentary about ancient times. And, of course, daydreaming about the next story she'll tell...

Stay in touch!
laurengoffiganbooks@gmail.com

www.ingramcontent.com/pod-product-compliance
Lightning Source LLC
LaVergne TN
LVHW091718070526
838199LV00050B/2443